The Charmer

AMISH COUNTRY BRIDES

Jennifer Spredemann

Published in Indiana by *Blessed Publishing*.

www.jenniferspredemann.com

All Scripture quotations are taken from the *King James Version* of the *Holy Bible*.

Cover design by *iCreate Designs* ©

ISBN: 978-1-940492-53-7
10 9 8 7 6 5 4 3 2 1

Get a FREE short story as my thank you gift to you when you sign up for my newsletter here:
www.jenniferspredemann.com

BOOKS by JENNIFER SPREDEMANN

Learning to Love – Saul's Story
(Sequel to Chloe's Revelation)

AMISH BY ACCIDENT TRILOGY
Amish by Accident
Englisch on Purpose (Prequel to *Amish by Accident*)
Christmas in Paradise (Sequel to *Amish by Accident*) (co-authored with Brandi Gabriel)

AMISH SECRETS SERIES
An Unforgivable Secret - Amish Secrets 1
A Secret Encounter - Amish Secrets 2
A Secret of the Heart - Amish Secrets 3
An Undeniable Secret - Amish Secrets 4
A Secret Sacrifice - Amish Secrets 5 (co-authored with Brandi Gabriel)
A Secret of the Soul - Amish Secrets 6
A Secret Christmas – Amish Secrets 2.5 (co-authored with Brandi Gabriel)

AMISH BIBLE ROMANCES
An Amish Reward (Isaac)
An Amish Deception (Jacob)
An Amish Honor (Joseph)
An Amish Blessing (Ruth)
An Amish Betrayal (David)

AMISH COUNTRY BRIDES
The Trespasser (Amish Country Brides)
The Heartbreaker (Amish Country Brides)
The Charmer (Amish Country Brides)

NOVELETTES
Cindy's Story – An Amish Fairly Tale Novelette 1
Rosabelle's Story – An Amish Fairly Tale Novelette 2

OTHER
Love Impossible
Unlikely Santa

COMING 2020 (Lord Willing)
The Unexpected Christmas Gift (Amish Christmas Miracles Collection)
Sequel to *Unlikely Santa* (title to be determined)

BOOKS by J.E.B. SPREDEMANN
AMISH GIRLS SERIES
Joanna's Struggle
Danika's Journey
Chloe's Revelation
Susanna's Surprise
Annie's Decision
Abigail's Triumph
Brooke's Quest
Leah's Legacy
A Christmas of Mercy – Amish Girls Holiday

Unofficial Glossary
of Pennsylvania Dutch Words

Ach – Oh

Bann – Shunning

Boppli/Bopplin – Baby/Babies

Bruder/Brieder – Brother/Brothers

Bu – Boy

Daed/Dat – Dad

Dawdi – Grandfather

Denki – Thanks

Der Herr – The Lord

Dummkopp – Dummy

Englischer – A non-Amish person

Ferhoodled – Mixed up

Fraa – Wife

G'may – Members of an Amish fellowship

Gott – God

Gut – Good

Jah – Yes

Kapp – Amish head covering

Kinner – Children

Kumm – Come

Maed/Maedel – Girls/Girl

Mamm – Mom

Mei fraa – My wife

Ordnung – Rules of the Amish community

Rumspringa – Running around period for Amish youth

Schatzi – Sweetheart

Schnickelfritz – Stinker, mischievous child, term of endearment

Schweschder(n) – Sister(s)

Sehr gut – Very good

Wunderbaar – Wonderful

Author's Note

The Amish/Mennonite people and their communities differ one from another. There are, in fact, no two Amish communities exactly alike. It is this premise on which this book is written. I have taken cautious steps to assure the authenticity of Amish practices and customs. Old Order Amish and New Order Amish may be portrayed in this work of fiction and may differ from some communities. Although the book may be set in a certain locality, the practices featured in the book may not necessarily reflect that particular district's beliefs or culture. This book is purely fictional and built around a fictional community, even though you may see similarities to real-life people, practices, and occurrences.

We, as *Englischers*, can learn a lot from the Plain People and their simple way of life. Their hard work, close-knit family life, and concern for others are to be applauded. As the Lord wills, may this special culture continue to be respected and remain so for many centuries to come, and may the light of God's salvation reach their hearts.

ONE

"Oh, no!" Jenny Christner yelped as panic gripped her entire being. She swerved the vehicle sharply to the right at the last second, narrowly missing the Amish buggy and its occupants. She had been daydreaming again, which was why she hadn't seen the buggy heading straight toward her.

The hard right she'd made landed her vehicle in a ditch just off the shoulder. She stared blankly through her windshield, out at the slanted scenery, her mind whirling. *Oh, no! What will I do now?*

With her heart pounding louder than she could think, she rested her head on the steering wheel. Her entire body trembled. *I could've killed someone.* Complete shock kept her tears at bay. Attempting to slow her breathing, she allowed her eyes to close.

The sound of her door creaking open forced her attention to the young Amish man responsible for the

action. She sensed stress and fury in his movements—
something she was all-too familiar with.

"What on earth do you think you're—" he'd
stopped mid-sentence when her eyes met his. He
blinked. "*Ach*, you—you're Amish? Why are you...?"
A deep frown etched into his face.

His eyes, blue like the color of the deep sea, pierced
hers. She could hardly look away.

"I'm sorry. I didn't see you." It was the truth. Well,
she hadn't seen him until it was nearly too late. Her
hands still shook so she stuffed them between the seat
and her legs.

He hung his head in what appeared to be regret.
"*Nee*, I'm sorry. I should have asked if you are okay."
His tone now gentle, he shook his head. "I was just—"

"I know. I completely understand. I could have
killed you. You have every right to be angry with me.
It was my fault. I wasn't paying attention."

"Why not?"

"I just...I have a lot on my mind right now." That
had been the understatement of the year.

"You're not from around here, are you?"

"No." Hopefully her simple answer would suffice.
Because she wasn't ready or willing to go into the
details of her chaotic life.

He frowned as he studied her. "Are you *sure* you're

all right?" He reached his hand toward her as though to touch her brow, then must've thought better of it. "You...you're injured."

"*Nee*, I'm fine, really."

"But you—"

"This isn't from the accident." She rubbed the ugly bruise on her eyebrow. She prayed he wouldn't ask her where she'd gotten it from. The acceptable response, Atlee insisted, was that she'd stepped on a rake which had sprung upward and smacked her in the eye.

She'd been smacked alright. But it hadn't been a rake. And she'd grown tired of lying to people.

She had to change the subject quickly before this man thought on it too long. "I need to get this car out of the ditch. Does it look like I can drive it out?" She doubted the words even as she uttered them.

"*Nee*." He pointed down the road. "My brother lives just up ahead. We can hook up his team and come pull you out."

"That would be great." Her eyes followed as he made his way around the vehicle.

"*Ach*, you have a tire down. It'll need to be fixed before you can drive anywhere." He scratched the faint stubble on his chin. "Why don't you come with me to Silas and Kayla's, and my brother and I can come back and pull your car out?"

"Oh. Are you sure?"

"*Jah.*"

"Okay." She momentarily deliberated over which items she'd bring with her. She opted for just her purse. Her suitcase should be fine unattended on the back floorboard for a few moments. This country road didn't appear to have much traffic. She'd only passed one other car on the entire stretch, and then this man's buggy.

He nodded briefly and extended a hand for her to climb out of the vehicle. She shook her head, not all that eager to make physical contact with a strange man. He led the way across the street to his spring buggy. As soon as she was situated next to him, he set the horse in motion with a faint jostling of the reins. He led the horse in a U-turn, and started toward the opposite direction from which he'd been headed. She closed her eyes as the clip-clop echoed on the asphalt. *This* was one thing she loved about the Plain life. The slow pace. The serenity. She'd missed this, although it had only been a couple of days since she'd been behind the reins. It seemed like a world away now.

She sighed deeply and took comfort in the fact that Atlee wasn't privy to her whereabouts. But it was only a matter of time until he found her. And he *would* find her. Of that, she was certain. The thought made her shiver.

"You okay?" The concern in this man's gaze made her feel like he might be someone she could trust.

But she'd once trusted Atlee too, and look where that had gotten her. "*Jah.*"

He seemed to study her, as if his eyes boring into her could reveal all her secrets. "If you're cold, I've got a blanket just in the back." He twisted slightly and reached over the seat with his free hand, then offered her a tattered quilt.

She swallowed, gratefulness filling her heart at his thoughtful ways. "*Denki.*"

"I'm Paul Miller, by the way."

She momentarily thought of making up a name for herself. *No more lies.* "I'm Jenny." Hopefully, her first name would suffice.

"Where were you headed?"

"*Ach.*" She shrugged, pulling the quilt around her shoulders. "I didn't really have a destination in mind." Had that been the wrong thing to say? Goodness, it was hard to think with those captivating eyes probing her.

"You are still Plain, *ain't so*?" His brow furrowed as he glanced at her.

She nodded.

"And your *g'may* allows for driving cars?"

"*Nee.*"

"I have a hundred questions in my head right now." He examined her thoughtfully. "Your eyebrow. If that wasn't from the accident, then—"

"I'd rather not talk about that." She shook her head and sighed. "I'm sorry. It's just complicated."

His lips turned down, clearly not satisfied with her answer. "What are you planning to do about your car?"

Right. Her car. Well, technically not hers. She needed to call the owner—one of their family's taxi drivers—so he wouldn't report it stolen. But how could she do that without alerting Atlee to her whereabouts? Another situation she hadn't intended getting herself into. "I don't know. I haven't thought that far."

"Where are you staying tonight?"

She grimaced. She really should have thought out her plan better. With the little money she had in her purse, she wouldn't get far. She'd planned on spending it on gas and sleeping in the car until she could find a decent-paying job to earn enough money to rent a small apartment or maybe just a room. It had sounded like a good idea at the time. But now?

"Let me guess. You haven't thought that far?"

"*Nee.*"

"Are you sure you don't want to talk about it?

6

Maybe sharing with someone else will help you come up with a solution." *Ach*, he wasn't one to give up easy.

Fine. She'd lay it out for him. "I need a job and a place to stay. Do you know where I can get that?"

"Well, not off the bat. But I could ask around. Maybe talk to my *bruder* and sister-in-law. They might know of something."

"I would appreciate that." She blew out an elongated breath and folded her hands in her lap. She would be safe here. At least, for a little while. Maybe.

TWO

Paul stole a quick glance at the beautiful, yet mysterious, young woman perched on the bench seat next to him. He guessed her to be near his own age, possibly a tad bit younger. He hoped she'd be staying for a while. He'd love to get to know her better.

No, no, you would not! He chastised himself. He'd been casually courting Amy Troyer over the past couple of months. But honestly, he wasn't all that attracted to her. There had been no special connection between them.

But this woman—Jenny. Wow! Not just wow, but *wow*! He didn't think he'd ever been so attracted to someone. Her hair color. Her eyes. Her lips. He should *not* be thinking about her lips. Should. Not.

Get it together, Paul!

He wished he would have helped her into the

buggy. At least then, he could've been close to her, maybe even could've touched her hand, which he imagined to be soft and delicate in comparison with his own. Not that she would have actually allowed that. She seemed pretty reserved.

A gentle breeze lifted the scent of something sweet to his nostrils. He was quite certain Jenny wore perfume. It was something he'd noticed when he'd yanked her door open after the accident. Oh, but he'd acted like a *dummkopp*. He couldn't have helped his ire, though. She'd nearly killed them both.

He flipped the switch to turn his signal on and swung a left into the familiar lane. As they moved past his brother's small store, memories flooded his mind of when his brother Silas first met his *fraa*. He'd thought his brother had lost his mind, to even entertain the thought of marrying an *Englisch* woman. But somehow, *Der Herr* had worked it out.

"Oh, would you mind stopping here? I'd like to make a phone call, if you think they won't mind."

He pulled the reins tight just past the phone shanty.

Jenny scrambled down from the buggy before he had a chance to offer assistance. "You don't have to wait. I can walk to the house."

"It's no problem. I'll wait."

She nodded, crossed the driveway, and stepped into the small phone shed.

Paul jumped down so he could assist her return entrance.

A moment later, she stepped out of the shanty. The sides of her lips engraved a frown into her cheeks. What load did she carry upon her narrow shoulders? Whatever it was, he hoped he could lighten it for her. He wished he could kiss that worry away.

Kiss? Nee. Oh, man. He had it bad. There was no way Silas wouldn't notice. And there was no way Silas would let him live it down. Not after all the flak he'd given his brother over Kayla.

He held out his hand for Jenny to take. She stopped momentarily and stared at his hand, then at him. No doubt she thought him *ab im kopp*. His grin widened and he winked. "A gentleman always assists a lady."

She giggled and allowed him to take her hand. The sound of her mirth was music to his ears. If only he could get her to smile more.

"And what should I have called you out on the road?" She sat on the buggy's bench seat, smoothing out her dress.

He ducked his head. "Again, I apologize for my rude behavior. It won't happen again." He jostled the reins and guided Blackie to the hitching post.

Once again, he hurried to Jenny's side of the carriage to offer a hand. He knew Blackie would stand in place, so he didn't worry about him moving.

"*Denki.*" She grinned.

Jenny stood in front of him, surveying the property, as he quickly wrapped the leather reins around the post. He looked up just as Silas approached.

"I see my baby brother's back. And he brought his—" Silas stopped talking when Paul stepped behind Jenny and made a throat-slashing motion with his hand, furiously pressing his lips together and shaking his head.

Silas's gaze moved to Jenny and he continued, "Oh, I thought you were—"

Paul shook his head almost violently, again using the throat cutting gesture, hoping his dense brother would finally get the hint. If Paul had *any* possible chance with a woman as gorgeous as Jenny, it was best she didn't know he'd been courting someone. "This is Jenny. Jenny, this is Silas. We had an accident out on the road and her car is in a ditch." He rushed on. "Can we hitch up the team and go pull the car out for her?"

"Uh...sure?" A puzzled look crossed Silas's face and he glanced back and forth from Paul to Jenny.

Paul needed to get Silas out of there before he said something Paul would regret.

"I'm Paul's big brother, by the way." Paul didn't miss the trace smirk forming on his brother's lips.

Jenny smiled. Thankfully, she'd seemed oblivious to their silent communication. "Nice to meet you."

"Is it okay if she stays here with Kayla and the *kinner* while we bring her car up to the house?" He gestured toward the road with his head.

"*Jah*, of course. Kayla's just inside." He glanced toward the house. "I'll go tell her you're here." He looked from Jenny to Paul once again, his brow furrowing, before heading into their family's dwelling.

Paul sighed in relief as Silas disappeared.

Jenny turned to him. "You two look a lot alike."

"We do?"

"Well, minus your brother's beard. But your eyes..." She immediately moved her gaze from his to the ground.

Were her cheeks darkening? *Ach*, so she'd noticed him too. Perfect. Well, *almost* perfect.

He needed to let Amy know he wouldn't be taking her home anymore. Practically speaking, he and Amy had never been serious. As far as he knew, he never gave Amy any indication otherwise. He'd never considered her to be the one for him, just someone to ride with him after the singings. He was pretty sure Amy felt the same way, although she'd never said so.

They'd never even discussed it, really. He liked Amy as a friend, but there had been no spark between them. Nothing like he felt when he'd been with Jenny—all of twenty minutes.

Was he being too presumptuous in hoping he'd get the chance to court her? He was willing to take the chance. One thing he knew was that he wouldn't be courting two girls at once. That would be asking for disaster.

He didn't know if it was the ginger tones in her hair or the spattering of freckles across her nose or the way her eyes reflected the green of her dress, but he had trouble prying his eyes off of her.

Was she *the one* for him? Was that why he felt this way? Or was that even a thing? Maybe he should ask Silas about how he'd felt when he met his first wife, then Kayla. Did they feel an instant attraction? Or was it something they'd eventually built up to as they got to know one another? And did it even make a difference?

All he knew was that he'd never felt so strongly about someone.

Atlee paced the barn, shaking his head. The nerve of Jenny leaving him here to look like a complete idiot. She'd been more cunning than he'd ever believed her to be. He'd done nothing but show her devotion, and he expected no less from her. He certainly hadn't counted on her skipping town—yesterday of all days!

He would *not* tolerate it. Jenny belonged to him now and he wasn't about to let her go for anyone or anything. He had to find her. Or maybe it would be better just to wait her out.

She wouldn't be gone forever. *Nee*, she would return. Wouldn't she? *Ach*, but what if she didn't? What if she stayed away for *gut*? He didn't know how she could. She didn't know anyone out there in the world. His Jenny, out there in the wicked world with all its sin and pleasures and enticements.

Or maybe she did know someone and she'd been hiding it from him. *Ach*, that was not acceptable.

Nee, he had to find her. He had to bring her into submission, like a *gut* Amish woman should be. He knew that she didn't like it when he had to correct her. But it was for her own *gut*. He had to find her for her own *gut*. He would protect her from *der welt*.

He tossed his head from side to side, working out the stress, then popped his knuckles. He'd do his hundred push-ups, then go for an hour jog. That should help release some of the tension he was feeling.

One thing he knew for sure—Jenny *would* be back with him, one way or another.

THREE

Paul's brother emerged from the house with an Amish woman at his side, whom Jenny presumed was his *fraa*. "Kayla," Silas said, "this is Jenny. She's the one that was in an accident, if I understand correctly."

"*Jah.*" Jenny grimaced, ducking her head, thoroughly embarrassed by her driving mishap. Surely these people would be wondering why she, an Amish woman, was behind the wheel of an *Englisch* vehicle. She hated lying, but she didn't know if she could trust these people or not.

"Would you like to come inside for tea or coffee?" Kindness radiated from Kayla's face. Her smile set Jenny's mind at ease.

"I would appreciate that. *Denki.*" Jenny glanced back at Paul.

He smiled and nodded. "Silas and I probably won't be too long. Enjoy yourself."

She found herself drawn to Paul's easygoing ways. He felt...*comfortable*? But she was wise enough now to know one couldn't depend on feelings. Just because something felt one way that didn't mean that it was. She sighed. Was it even fair to judge Paul by Atlee's actions? She couldn't allow herself to be deceived again, though.

She followed Kayla into the quiet house.

Kayla glanced at her as they walked through the living area toward the kitchen. "The *bopplin* are sleeping right now. Our oldest, Bailey, is at school," she explained in hushed tones.

"You have three *kinner* then?"

"*Ach.*" She placed a hand over her abdomen, evidencing a small but noticeable bump. "And one on the way, *Gott* willing." Happiness shined in her eyes.

Jenny yearned for that kind of contentment. What would it be like to be happily married to someone whom you loved with all your heart, as Kayla obviously did Silas?

"You may have a seat." Kayla gestured toward the dining table as she filled a kettle with water.

"Oh, no. I'll help," she insisted. "Where are your cups?"

Kayla gestured toward a cabinet. "There."

Jenny opened the cabinet and reached up to get the

two plain mugs nearest her.

Kayla gasped. "*Ach*, what happened to your arm?"

Jenny quickly attempted to cover up her wrist, avoiding Kayla's probing eyes. "It's...uh...nothing." She hastily set the mugs on the table. Her face felt hot all of a sudden. She'd been a *dummkopp* to expose her arms. She'd forgotten all about the bruises Atlee left.

Kayla sat at the table and gestured for Jenny to sit too. "I understand if you don't want to talk about it." Kayla's lips turned down. "I had a friend in high school whose boyfriend was abusive. She didn't want to say anything either."

"High school?" Jenny frowned. She'd never heard of Amish attending high school, but maybe this *g'may* allowed for higher education.

Kayla smiled. "I used to be *Englisch*."

"*Ach*, really? I would have never guessed."

"*Jah*." Kayla pinned her with a probing gaze. "Abuse happens everywhere."

Jenny shook her head. "I hate to talk about it. Nobody believes you anyway." She fought the tears that threatened to manifest themselves.

Kayla reached across the table and placed her hand over Jenny's. "If you tell me it's the truth, I'll believe you. No judgment. I'm here to listen if you want to talk." She squeezed her hand, then let go.

"I wouldn't even know where to start."

"How about right now? How did you end up here? Where were you going? You were driving a car, right? Are you still in *rumspringa*?"

"No, I'm not. And I didn't really have a specific destination in mind." She sighed. "As a matter of fact, the car doesn't belong to me. I shouldn't have taken it, but I was so desperate to get away from him."

"From who?" Kayla stood from the table to retrieve the steaming kettle on the stove.

"His name is Atlee." She absentmindedly stroked the mug in her hands.

Kayla set the kettle on a potholder in the center of the table and offered her a choice of a variety of tea bags from a wooden box. Jenny chose chamomile and dropped the bag into her mug. She needed something relaxing right now.

Kayla poured water over each of their tea bags, then covered the cups with a saucer to steep. "Is that an Amish name? I'm sorry if I sound ignorant. I've only been Plain for about four and a half years. I don't recall ever hearing that name."

"Yes, it's an Amish name."

"Who is he to you? A boyfriend?"

"He was, *jah*." Technically not a lie.

"Did he give you that bruise over your eye too?"

Jenny lifted a half-smile. "That's supposed to be from stepping on a rake."

Kayla shook her head and rolled her eyes. "Did anyone actually believe that explanation?"

She shrugged. "People believe what they want to."

"I'm sorry." Kayla shook her head. "So, you don't have any place to go?"

"I had planned to just park somewhere and sleep in the car. And then find a job so I could save up enough money to buy different clothes and get a place to stay."

Kayla's expression widened. "You were going to sleep in your car? That would be really dangerous."

"Well, it probably wouldn't be any more dangerous than staying where I was. And it's not my car. I eventually need to get it back to the owner."

A concerned look flashed across Kayla's face. "You didn't *steal* the car, did you?"

Her hands fidgeted. "I...I'm borrowing it."

"*Jah*, but does the owner know?"

"*Nee*. I mean, maybe he might. I tried to call just now but I didn't get anyone." She gestured toward where she guessed the phone shanty was located. It was difficult to tell from inside the house. She was all twisted around, being unfamiliar with her surroundings.

"How long have you had it?"

21

"Just since yesterday."

Kayla grimaced. "There's a good chance they've reported it stolen. If they did, the police are likely looking for you. Probably wouldn't have been a good idea to sleep in a stolen car."

Jenny covered her face. "I know. I've thought of that. I just, I don't know what to do. And now the car is…" This time, she couldn't help the tears.

"I have an idea. I'll have to talk to my husband about it first." She tapped her fingers on the table. "Maybe we can help you."

Help? Hope surged in her gut. *Ach*, if Kayla could offer some kind of solution, she'd be indebted to her. "I never thought my life would be like this. I didn't expect to ever leave my family and my community."

"I know what you mean. I never planned on getting pregnant at sixteen and having a baby out-of-wedlock. And I certainly never thought I'd end up Amish." Kayla laughed. "Life can be crazy. I'm just glad that God knows what's going on."

Jenny couldn't hide her shock. "Really?"

"Yeah, I had thought Bailey and I ended up here by coincidence, but it most definitely was *not* a coincidence. I have no doubt God was orchestrating my every move, clearing a path for my feet, leading me straight to Silas and this community. It was the craziest thing. I'll tell you all about it one day when we have plenty of time."

"Wow. That's sounds interesting." She wasn't sure how long she'd even be in this area. But the fact that Kayla had reached out a hand of friendship to her, a mere stranger, made her long to stay. Was staying in an Amish community even a good idea, though?

"Looking back on it now, it was nothing short of amazing. But at the time, it was scary. I had no idea what I was doing. I had no idea what God was doing. I don't even know if I believed in Him at the time. I certainly didn't trust Him. But now I *know* He is in control and can be trusted. But it took a while for me to see that."

"Kind of sounds like my life right now. I think *Der Herr* knows, maybe, but I have no idea what's going to become of all this."

"I have a feeling we might have a lot in common." Kayla smiled, then stood from the table. "I like honey in my tea. Would you like some too?" She held up a plastic bear container.

"Sure. Thanks." Jenny squeezed out her tea bag, set it on the saucer, then took the honey bear from Kayla, along with a stirring spoon.

"The guys should be coming back soon."

"Kayla." Jenny briefly touched her hand, her eyes

pleading. "You won't say anything, will you?"

"Not if you don't want me to. But I think Silas and Paul should probably know. They're going to have a lot of questions." Kayla studied her for a moment. "But I can be vague."

"I appreciate it. Truly."

FOUR

"Alright, baby *bruder*, spill it." Silas maneuvered the team of draft horses out onto the road.

"What?" Paul played dumb.

"Oh, no." Silas pointed a finger at him. "You are *not* getting by without telling me what is going on. What happened? Do you know this girl from somewhere?"

"Nope. Just met her after we almost crashed."

"And?" Silas rotated his hand, prodding him to continue.

"And what?"

"You're obviously infatuated with her."

Paul sighed in contentment, a slow smile creeping over his face. "She's gorgeous, *ain't so*?"

"Can't say I noticed. I only have eyes for one woman, *bruder*."

Paul shook his head. "But you *do* have eyes. And I know you saw her."

"Ah, she's almost as pretty as Kayla, I guess."

"Almost?!"

"You don't have to shout. I'm sitting right next to you, *bruder*." Silas chuckled.

"She's the most beautiful girl I've ever seen."

"You think?"

"No, not think. I *know*." He rubbed his hands on his pants. "What do I do about it?"

"What do you mean?"

"Well, I don't want her to leave. How can I keep her here? How can I talk her into allowing me to court her?"

"Where is she going?"

"I don't know." Paul shrugged.

"Where is she from?"

"I don't know."

Silas turned to stare at him. "What *do* you know about her?"

"Her name is Jenny." He grinned like a fool.

"Jenny what?"

"I don't know."

Silas hooted, slapping his hat on his pant leg.

"What? What's so funny?"

"You're convinced you want to marry this girl and you don't even know her name."

"I told you, it's Jenny." Why was it taking so long

to get to the vehicle? Oh, *jah*, draft horses. Strong as anything, but slow to a fault. He was used to his speedy buggy horse, Blackie, sired from a champion racehorse.

"Are you *sure* about that?"

"It's what she said anyhow."

"Why are you so interested in her? There are plenty of *maed* in our district you can court. Why her? And what about Amy? I thought you were courting her."

"Amy is ancient history. Or, she will be after Sunday. She knows I only like her as a friend."

"You think so, huh?"

"*Jah*, of course."

"How long have you been courting her?"

He shrugged. "About three months, I guess."

"*Ach*, Paul."

"What?"

"You can't do that to a *maedel*."

"Do what?"

"Court her for three months, letting her think that she has a chance with you, then dump her like yesterday's garbage."

"I don't treat girls like garbage. And I was going to tell her nicely."

"*Ach*, Paul." Silas's tone grated on his nerves.

"Stop saying that," he spat out.

"You know you're going to break her heart, right?"

"Whose?"

Silas rolled his eyes. "Amy's. I've seen the way she looks at you. She's going to be devastated."

"She is?"

"I never knew you were this clueless. I see you need a little training in the courting department from your experienced older *bruder*."

Paul snorted. "You've courted all of two women, both whom you married. I've taken more girls home in my buggy than I can count on my fingers."

"See, that's what I mean. You're doing it all wrong. Do you not care that you're going to hurt Amy deeply?"

Paul lifted his hat and sifted his hair through his fingers. "Look, I've never made her any promises, never even kissed her. We just drove around and talked, played games, and had snacks together."

"*Jah*, I know what courting is. Usually that continues until you talk about marriage and a life together. That's how it was with Sadie Ann and me."

"Sadie Ann." Paul sighed. "Do you ever miss her?"

"*Jah*, of course. She was my first love. And the *mudder* of my first *boppli*—one I never got to rock to sleep." Silas's eyes glazed over.

"I'm sorry for bringing it up."

Silas shoved away a tear. "*Nee*, don't be. It's *gut* to keep them in memory. They existed, and I wouldn't want to ever forget their existence. They meant the world to me at the time. Losing them was the hardest thing I've ever been through."

Paul squeezed his brother's shoulder. "I know. I remember. It was hard for all of us."

"But *Gott* was *gut* to me. He brought Kayla and Bailey into my life when I least expected it. And now we have Judah and Shiloh too. They've helped my heart to heal."

"And another one on the way too, *ain't so*?"

"*Ach, Gott* willing." Silas smiled, his face darkening slightly. "So you've noticed."

"*Jah.* Kind of hard not to. How much longer does Kayla have?"

"Three months yet."

"That must be exciting to hold your own flesh and blood. Little ones you've created with the woman you're crazy about."

"*Jah*, it is. A gift from *Der Herr* for sure and certain."

"I want that someday."

"With Jenny?" Silas smirked.

He clasped his hands together and blew out a breath. "Maybe. That would be amazing." Just the thought...*wow*.

"You should get to know her first. It's better to dwell in a corner of the housetop than with a brawling woman in a wide house."

Paul chuckled. "I doubt she's a brawling woman."

"*Jah*, but is she virtuous?"

He turned serious. "From what I've seen so far, she seems kind and gentle. One that someone without much sense would take advantage of." He clenched his hands into fists and growled.

"What? You think someone has taken advantage of her?"

"Did you see the bruise above her eyebrow? It wasn't from the accident. She won't tell me how she got it. What does that tell you?"

"Is she running, do you think?"

"I think it's a very *gut* possibility. She said she doesn't know where she's going. And she's looking for a job and a place to stay."

"I don't think *Mamm* would want her staying in their *dawdi haus*, if that's what you're thinking." Silas flicked a glance in his direction.

"*Jah*, I know. Especially if she knows I've taken a shine to her." Paul sighed. "I love *Mamm*, but..."

"Speak no further. I totally understand. Do you remember when I brought Kayla home for the first time?"

Paul laughed out loud. "How could I forget? That was classic."

"Maybe. But *Mamm* was madder than a pack of riled coyotes."

"Well, you can't really blame her. Kayla was *Englisch*."

"*Jah*." He scratched his beard. "You know, I'm thinking Kayla could probably use Jenny's help with the *bopplin* and with making goods to sell in the store. I reckon she could work there too, but I can only pay her part time. We don't pull in a whole lot of income, just enough to keep it going and make it worth our while."

"I'm sure she would appreciate anything she can get."

"I'll need to discuss it with Kayla first."

"Of course."

They finally pulled up to Jenny's vehicle. Silas jumped down, knowing the gentle giants would stay put unless they were spooked—a rare occurrence on this country road. As a matter of fact, the accident was the most excitement this road had seen since a neighbor's house caught fire a couple years back. "Time to get this thing rigged up and pull it back home."

It was going to be a long afternoon. *Jah*, he'd probably see Jenny sooner if he walked back to the house.

FIVE

"It looks like they're back," Kayla called from the window. "They're taking the car into the barn."

"Oh, good. Do you think I should find out what's wrong with it before I call the owner, or would it be better to call him right away?" Jenny worried her lip. She didn't even want to think of that conversation, but it needed to happen.

"I'd say call them so they won't worry and have the police out looking for the car." Kayla returned to the table. "Silas and Paul might be able to tell you what's wrong with it. Do you think it was damaged? Did you hit anything?"

"Not that I know of, just the ditch."

"I wouldn't worry too much, then."

"I don't know how I'm going to get it back to the owner. I don't want to go back there. I don't want Atlee to know where I am."

Kayla pressed her lips together. "We'll figure something out. Don't worry."

"*Denki*. For everything."

"That's what friends are for, *ain't so*?" The second a baby's cry pierced the air, Kayla's head shot up. "*Ach*, it sounds like the *kinner* are up from their naps. I'll be right back."

"Okay." She watched Kayla disappear down a hallway.

If only she could stay here and make a life for herself. Maybe she could just hide out here. Maybe begin a new life. Nobody knew her here except Paul, Kayla, and Silas. Too bad she'd told Paul her real name. If she'd made something else up, it would be easier. As it was, though, if she attended church with them, she'd surely encounter a scribe for one of the Plain publications. Or a scribe would enquire of her through someone else. And if that happened, it would likely be printed in The Budget or elsewhere.

All it would take is for someone in her home district to read about it and Atlee would know. And he'd be on her doorstep. She couldn't let that happen.

Maybe she should just be upfront with Paul and his family. Maybe they could offer advice or a solution to her problem. Because if she didn't, she wouldn't be staying here long at all. And maybe she shouldn't.

Because if Paul offered a relationship of any kind, she'd be tempted to accept. And she was in no position to begin a new relationship with a man—not even handsome Paul Miller.

Nee, sooner or later her past would be made known. And at that point...no, she didn't want to think about it. They could never know about her past.

The moment Paul stepped into the house, his stomach began flip-flopping.

"*Onkel* Paul! *Onkel* Paul!" Judah ran in his direction.

Paul stooped down and gathered his young nephew into his arms, his belly flutters immediately dispelling.

"Hey, Jude. Did you miss your *onkel*?" He tickled the little one's tummy, which produced a fit of giggles.

"*Ach*, I get no attention from my *kinner* when *Onkel* Paul's around," Silas lamented as he walked past.

"That's 'cuz you're old and no fun." Paul chuckled.

"Well, once the responsibility of a family is placed on your shoulders, you'll understand why I'm exhausted at the end of the day."

Paul's brow shot up. "*Jah*, but not too exhausted

for some things." He made a rounded gesture over his belly.

Unfortunately, it had happened at the same time Kayla and Jenny chose to walk into the room. All four of the adults flushed, but Paul was certain his face must be the color of the beets in *Mamm's* garden.

Kayla turned to Jenny, with little Shiloh in her arms. "See what I mean about the two of them trying to embarrass each other? It looks like that one backfired, Paul," she teased.

"I, uh, *jah.*" He bowed his head. "Sorry." He set little Judah back on the floor.

"More! More!" Judah protested.

"More? You want more?" Paul made a funny face, then grabbed Judah by the suspenders and gently wrestled him to the floor. He pulled up the little one's shirt and blew noisily on his tummy, producing another round of uncontrollable giggles.

When he glanced up, Jenny's face was aglow with pleasure. He could get used to that look.

Paul's eyes roamed the room.

"I think your *bruder* and sister-in-law are talking in the other room." Jenny smiled.

"Did you and Kayla have a nice time?"

"*Jah.*"

"*Gut.*" They stared at each other for several seconds

until Judah demanded his attention once again.

Kayla and Silas emerged from their bedroom. Silas looked to both of them. "Let's talk at the kitchen table?"

"Okay." Jenny nodded.

"We'll wait until Kayla gets the little ones settled with their snacks."

"Do you need help?" Jenny offered.

"*Ach, nee.*" Kayla quickly spread out a blanket on the floor and set one-and-a-half-year-old Shiloh down next to Judah, along with some crackers and toys. They'd be occupied for a little while, but Paul noticed that Kayla kept the *kinner* in her line of vision.

Once Kayla joined them at the table, Silas began speaking. He turned his focus to Jenny. "Kayla and I have discussed your situation. You are welcome to stay here with us to help Kayla with the *kinner* and our store, if that suits you."

Tears surfaced in Jenny's eyes. "That would be *wunderbaar. Denki.*"

"We won't be able to pay you much—"

Jenny held up her hand. "You don't need to pay me. I will gladly work for free if I can stay here."

"*Nee.* We will pay you something," Silas insisted. His gaze turned sober. "Will you join the *g'may?*"

"*Ach.*" She shook her head. "I don't...I haven't

figured that part out." She looked from Silas to Kayla, then glanced briefly at Paul. "Did...did Kayla tell you anything?"

"About the abusive ex-boyfriend?" Silas's brow rose.

Paul stole a glance at Jenny but didn't want her to feel uncomfortable.

She hung her head. "*Jah*."

"She didn't have to," Silas asserted. "Paul and I already suspected as much."

Paul's gaze lowered to Jenny and he briefly reached over and gently squeezed her hand. "You're safe here."

"I don't know if I am." She shook her head, worry wrinkling her forehead.

"What do you mean?" Silas asked.

"I'm sure and certain that a scribe will report my visit. Word will get back to home. And Atlee will show up on our doorstep. I'm sure of it."

Atlee. So that was the jerk's name. Anger pumped through Paul's veins. He clenched then unclenched his hands. If the man *ever* came near Jenny again...Paul might just lose his Amish testimony.

Kayla and Silas looked at each other and frowned.

"I have an idea." Paul stood up. "What if..." He glanced at the children then realized he was being too loud. He sat back down and lowered his voice. "What if nobody knew it was Jenny?"

Silas tossed a puzzled look in his direction. "What do you mean?"

"Just hear me out. What if Jenny was an old *Englisch* friend of Kayla's from California? No one would ever know the difference. She could attend *g'may* in *Englisch* clothing as Kayla's friend."

Silas glanced at the *kinner*, then back at Paul. "So you'd want her...*us*...to live a lie?" He shook his head in disapproval.

"Come on, Silas. Do you have a better idea?" Paul challenged.

Silas shrugged, rubbing his beard.

"I think it's a great idea, Paul," Kayla chimed in. "Like the Witness Protection Program."

"Thank you." Paul smiled at his sister-in-law. Finally, someone on his side.

Silas frowned at his *fraa*.

"Think about it. It's the perfect solution." Kayla reasoned, "Don't you remember the story in the Bible when Rahab hid the spies. It's the same thing, really. And if we can keep Jenny safe, I'm all for it."

"I don't know." Silas shook his head, discomfort filling his features.

"What does Jenny think? She's the one at risk here." Kayla smiled at Jenny.

Jenny pulled her bottom lip in between her teeth. "I think it *might* be a *gut* idea. I don't like to lie, but..."

"And none of us do." Paul pinned an accusing gaze on his brother.

Silas raised his hands. "Hey, I just want to please *Der Herr*. And I have my family to think about. Lay off, Paul."

"I don't want to cause any problems." Jenny shook her head. "I can leave."

Ire rose in Paul's veins. *If Silas ran her off...*

"*Nee*." Silas said. "It's okay. Paul's right. This is probably the best solution."

"Finally, you agree." Paul blew out a breath, releasing his frustration. He then turned to Kayla. "Do you still have any of your *Englisch* clothes?"

"*Nee*. I donated them to the thrift store."

"Well, it looks like the two of you will need to make a trip to the store to find some *Englisch* clothes, then," Silas said. "Should probably do it before Bailey gets home from school. If not, you'll be hard pressed keeping her quiet."

Paul stood up. "I'll go call a driver."

"I can watch the *kinner* while you two do your thing," Silas offered.

Jenny smiled her gratitude. "*Denki* ever so much to all of you. You don't know how much this means."

Kayla looked at Jenny and winked. "It looks like I'm going to have to teach you how to be *Englisch*."

Silas shrugged. "Well, you've learned to become a *gut* Amish woman."

Paul moved to the door, but Silas caught him just before he walked outside.

Silas pulled him close and whispered in his ear, "Good luck convincing *Mamm* to support you courting an *Englisch* woman." Silas chuckled.

He jabbed Silas in the side. "*Ach*, I hadn't thought of that. *Mamm* doesn't need to know."

"*Jah.* Sure." Silas laughed.

Paul shook his head, then walked out the door. On the other hand, courting in secret might be good. *Mamm* didn't need to know anything. He could occasionally take his meals here at Silas's, drive around with Jenny, and no one would be the wiser.

That is, if he could talk his niece Bailey into keeping her mouth closed.

Kayla pulled Jenny into her bedroom, away from where Silas now entertained the little ones. "Silas said Paul may have taken a shining to you."

Kayla's words and knowing smile caused Jenny's heart to flutter.

"*Ach*, you think?" She'd suspected as much, but to have someone else confirm it made it difficult to breathe. *Ach*, Paul was so handsome.

"Between you and me, I think Paul's a great guy. Good-looking like his brother. A lot of fun to be around. A little mischievous, but he has a big heart. And he's great with the kids." She winked. "Just don't tell him I said that. We give him a hard time. In case you haven't noticed, he and Silas have a thing going. I think it's called 'who can embarrass his brother the most?'" She laughed. "He'll make a good catch for someone. But I might be a little biased since I am married to his brother."

Jah, she'd seen Paul interacting with little Judah. He would likely make a *gut vatter*. She couldn't even imagine how Atlee would be with young *kinner*. She quaked just thinking about it. Paul, on the other hand, sounded like someone she could only dream about. But she didn't dare. Not with Atlee probably out there searching for her.

"I...probably shouldn't get into a relationship right now." She reached up and touched her brow.

"I'm sure it's hard to trust after that, ain't so?"

"I want to. But I once trusted someone else before. I just...I don't know."

"I totally understand. I was like that after what

happened with Bailey's father. I never dated again until I met Silas. I was afraid to. And of course, I had a baby to take care of. Maybe with time you'll be able to open your heart again."

"Maybe."

SIX

"How would you feel if we call you Sierra?" Glancing at Jenny, Kayla handed Shiloh off to Silas.

She smiled and shrugged. "I like it."

"There's actually a girl that I went to school with who had that name and you look a little like her."

"Sierra?" Silas eyed his *fraa*.

"*Jah*, you know. Like the Sierra Nevada mountain range that borders California and Nevada. "It's perfect. It builds authenticity."

"Whatever." Silas chuckled. "We'll need to tell Paul."

As if on cue, Paul entered the house. "The driver will be here in about five minutes. Are you two ready to go?" Paul's gaze met Jenny's and she smiled shyly.

"Yes, as a matter of fact, *Sierra* and I have everything we need." Kayla grinned.

"Sierra?" Paul's brow shot up and he fought a smile.

"Yes," Jenny chimed in. "You know, like the Sierra Nevada mountain range in California." She winked at Kayla.

"Mm...impressive." Paul nodded. "Nice to meet you, Sierra." He held out his hand for her to shake and winked.

"Nice to meet you too, Paul." She tittered, then shook her head. "This is going to take a little getting used to."

"We'll introduce her to the driver as Sierra. Tell her that she's my friend from California and wanted to dress Amish."

"Sounds convincing enough to me. But I must say that I prefer Jenny." Paul held her gaze in a caress, and his brow rose slightly.

She felt her cheeks warming at his open show of interest. Paul Miller, the charmer, was going to be a difficult one to say no to.

"Jenny no longer exists." Kayla shot him a look of warning, then glanced at the *kinner*.

"*Jah*. Right." He turned to Jenny. "So, tell me about California, Sierra."

"Uh..." She glanced at Kayla, uncertainty filled her. "What would you like to know?"

"What is your favorite thing to do there?"

"Um...go to the beach?" She looked to Kayla, who approved by nodding.

"What's your favorite beach?" Paul challenged.

"Uh..." Jenny looked to Kayla for help.

"Santa Cruz. We loved to go to Santa Cruz because they have a boardwalk, with games and amusement park rides. But the water there is cold. Southern California is the place to go if you want to go into the ocean, because it's warm there. But there are usually a lot of people and the freeways are really congested, so we prefer Central and Northern California beaches."

"Ah..." Paul nodded. "Santa Cruz, huh? An amusement park? Sounds like the devil's playground."

"What?" Kayla play-slapped his arm. "It is not. There's nothing wrong with having a little fun now and then."

"I don't think the deacon would agree with you on that," he teased.

"Well, the deacon isn't God."

"I don't think he claims to be." Paul was obviously having fun with this.

"Whatever."

Silas stepped near with Shiloh in his arms. "You aren't giving my *fraa* a hard time, are you, *bruder*?"

"Me? Of course not!" Paul pretended to be

offended, causing Jenny to smile. He turned to her. "Where's your favorite place to eat in California?"

Worry furrowed Jenny's brow and her eyes begged Kayla for help once again.

"We love *In-N-Out Burger*. Especially the Animal Fries. Right, Sierra?"

"Yeah, of course, Animal Fries." She nodded and laughed, then turned to Kayla. "What are Animal Fries?"

"Remember? They have their special sauce on the fries with sautéed onions and cheese. Oh my, I'm dying for some just thinking about it. I think I need to talk Silas into taking me to California." She winked.

"*Ach*, having your friend Sierra here is beginning to get expensive." Silas chuckled.

"But I'm worth it, right?" Kayla's hip playfully bumped her husband's.

"Every penny." He grinned, his eyes sparkling with love.

"*Ach*, our ride is here." Kayla stepped on her tiptoes and kissed Silas on the cheek. She pointed to her husband and to Paul. "You two behave yourselves. And don't let the *kinner* out of your sight."

Silas chuckled. "Okay, *fraa*."

"Oh, no. We won't get into one little bit of trouble. Will we Silas?" Paul nudged his brother. "We'll just make some popcorn—"

"No popcorn," Kayla hollered from the door. "The babies can choke on it."

Jenny loved watching their banter. What would it be like to be part of this *wunderbaar* family?

"Let's go, Sierra." Kayla pulled her to the vehicle and they both slid into the back seat.

Paul, Silas, and the little ones stood at the door, waving them off. "Bye, Kayla. Bye Sierra."

Did Paul just wink at her again? *Ach.*

Kayla stood to the right of Jenny as they perused the racks of clothing. "I'm guessing you're about a size six or eight, so we'll look for pants in those sizes and you can try them on."

Jenny frowned. "Pants?"

Kayla moved close and lowered her voice. "You have to dress in *Englisch* clothes if you want people to think you're *Englisch*. We'll get you some shorts too, and maybe a cute skirt."

"I've never worn men's trousers, not even in *rumspringa*."

"Good. It will make it harder for people to notice you. I think we should get you some makeup too. You can drastically change your looks with cosmetics. It's a good thing I know how to apply it." Kayla grinned.

"This will be fun!"

Twenty minutes later, with a shopping cart full of clothes, they headed for the dressing room. As Jenny tried on each outfit, she hardly recognized herself. And she looked absolutely ridiculous with her hair pinned up in a *kapp* and wearing jeans and a t-shirt.

"Okay, you should definitely wear that home. Minus the *kapp*, of course." Kayla pulled out another outfit, prompting her to try it on.

Jenny glanced down at the aqua dress she'd tried on.

"Oh, my goodness, Sierra! You look so pretty in that."

"Do you think so?" Her hands fidgeted.

"So cute."

She briefly wondered what Paul would think.

"Paul won't be able to keep his eyes off you." Had Kayla read her mind? She snapped her fingers. "Okay, I want to see the other outfits on you. That pink shirt is so cute. *Ach*, I miss some of the clothes I used to wear."

"I'm not going to cause you to sin, am I?"

"You mean, because of the clothes?" Kayla smiled. "It's not a sin to wear *Englisch* clothes, even though the leaders might not agree. It's a sin to dress immodestly. Nothing we are getting is immodest."

Jenny mentally disagreed, but trusted Kayla's judgment. She used to be an *Englischer*, after all. Jenny picked up the next outfit Kayla laid out—denim shorts and a bright orange top.

"It's a culture thing, not a sin thing." Kayla looked over her outfit. "So cute. We need to get you some sandals to go with that."

"*Ach*, I feel like this will cost a lot of money."

"Don't worry about it. We're staying within our budget. That's why we came to the thrift store and not a department store."

"Budget?"

"Silas and Paul both gave me a twenty. Several of those items are on sale, so we'll only pay half price for them. It's awesome that we can get several cute outfits for the price of one pair of jeans at the department store. I love thrift store shopping."

Just the thought of these kind people helping her out caused tears to surface. They were virtually strangers—well, strangers who had become fast friends. "*Denki*."

""Thank you," Kayla reminded her she was an *Englischer* now. "That's what friends are for, right?"

"Right." She smiled.

"Now, let's get these clothes home so we can wash them. First, though, we'll need to stop at another store and buy you some makeup. I'll ask our driver to go by the dollar store. We'll get the most bang for our buck there." Kayla was certainly more *Englisch* than she was and it was obvious.

"Okay."

"It's fun doing these girly things, don't you think?"

"*Jah.*"

SEVEN

Jenny snipped the last tag off her thrift store purchases and handed them to Kayla, who promptly dropped them into the wringer washer. At Kayla's suggestion, she'd changed into one of the outfits during their shopping trip. Kayla reasoned that her daughter Bailey might be home from school and it would be best if she didn't suspect anything. Kayla also insisted on a trip to the hair salon. Not only had she taken her hair down, but they trimmed and styled it. Kayla applied a little bit of makeup to her face as well. Jenny couldn't help feeling like a foreigner in her own body.

She'd been disappointed to hear that Paul had returned home, and wondered when she would see him again. Truthfully, she wanted to see his reaction to her *Englisch* transformation.

Kayla's words pulled her from her thoughts.

"We're going to need to work on your speech. I'll teach you some *Englisch* phrases that the Amish don't use. You'll have to try to lose your accent. Absolutely no Amish words. They will give you away. And when others are speaking it, you need to pretend like you have no clue what they are saying."

"Okay. I'm going to try not to say too many things when I'm around people other than you, Silas, and Paul."

"That's not a bad idea. And practice your posture. I've noticed that Amish tend to stoop a little more, which totally goes along with a submissive culture. You need to keep your head up. Like you're strong and confident. When no one is around, place a book on top of your head, put your shoulders back and try to walk erect. This will help with your posture."

Jenny giggled. "You want me to walk around with a book on my head?"

"I know it sounds funny, but it really works. A friend of mine was in modeling school and that was one of the things they had her do. Also, practice walking like this." Kayla moved to one end of the basement, then began walking across to the other side. "Place one foot in front of the other, and sway your hips slightly."

Jenny laughed again. *Ach*, what would Paul think? "I don't know."

"Just try it," Kayla encouraged.

She sighed. "Okay." She began walking, attempting to remember all Kayla had said.

"Remember, keep your head up. Don't look down or at the ground. Shoulders back. One foot in front of the other." Kayla coached.

"I feel really silly."

"Don't even think about it. You're an *Englischer*, remember? You have to walk the walk and talk the talk."

"Walk the walk. Talk the talk. That sounds *Englisch*." She moved back to the washer and began feeding her new clothing through the wringer.

"Coffee!" Kayla's hand flew into the air.

Jenny chuckled. "Coffee?"

"Yes, that is something *Englischers* are crazy over. You should talk about the fancy coffees you like to drink."

"I should? I do?"

"Okay. You just need to be familiar with the most popular drinks. So, a latte is a coffee drink that's made with strong coffee, called espresso, and steamed milk. A frappe or Frappuccino is a cold blended drink. Mocha fraps are the best. Mocha is coffee with chocolate. There's also a caramel macchiato. Those are really popular too. But they're crazy sweet." Kayla nodded. "Yeah, say things like 'crazy sweet.' That's totally an *Englisch* thing. Like 'that guy is crazy hot.' Of course, *I'd* be talking about Silas. Because he totally is."

"You really were an *Englischer*." Jenny laughed. "I don't think I can remember all that coffee stuff."

"Just say things like, I could really go for a mocha frap right now. Or, oh man! I'm dying for some animal fries."

Jenny frowned.

"Don't worry. I'll write you a list of things and you can practice."

"Alright."

"I better quit talking so much and help you get this laundry done. Silas is probably wondering what's taking us so long." She moved to take the rinsed and wrung out items and began placing them in the laundry basket to take outside and pin on the line. "By the way, Silas said Paul is joining us for supper tonight." A knowing look flashed across Kayla's face.

Jenny glanced down at her attire. She hoped Paul would be pleased with, as Kayla had put it, her '*Englisch* debut.'

As Paul maneuvered Blackie into his folks' driveway,

he puzzled over the extra buggy outside the barn. Did *Mamm* have company over today? It wasn't a sisters' day, otherwise Kayla would have been present. Had one of his older siblings come to visit?

When he came closer to the house, that's when he realized who the carriage belonged to. It was owned by the Troyer family, which meant Amy was likely here visiting with his sister Martha.

Good. Maybe he'd have a chance to talk to her about the young folks' gathering on Sunday. She needed to know that he wouldn't be driving her home. Or any other Amish *maedel*, for that matter. As a matter of fact, he didn't even plan on attending the event. Not that he would tell *her* that.

Nee, he'd be spending his free time at Silas's house. He needed more time with his nieces and nephew—at least that would be his excuse. In actuality, he'd be getting to know the beautiful Amish-turned-*Englisch* girl from California. It would be strange indeed seeing Jenny as the *Englisch* Sierra.

Ach, it seemed like he'd been daydreaming about her since the moment he first saw her. There had been something about her that drew him to her during that first encounter. He'd thought her beautiful, *jah*, but that hadn't been it.

It had been her eyes, he realized. They'd

held...something. A pain, an inexplicable sadness in their depths. A wariness, or fear, even. Then when he'd asked about the wound over her eye and she declined to answer, he knew. He'd felt an overwhelming urge to immediately gather her into his arms and protect her like a hen does her chicks.

It was almost like her spirit was injured. Who had done that to his sweet Jenny? What kind of man would use his *Gott*-given strength to intimidate and harm a gentle-hearted woman? He didn't want to think about what might happen if he ever came face-to-face with this monster. For sure and for certain, he would not be able to control his anger. He would not be able to keep true to the Amish ways. He would likely get shunned over his actions, if not put in jail. *Nee*, he could never come face-to-face with this man who had taken advantage of his precious *maedel*.

Ach, where had these evil thoughts come from? *Der Herr* would not be pleased with him right now, of that he was certain. But what was the solution? How could he get justice for Jenny?

But I say unto you, Love your enemies, bless them that curse you, do good to them that hate you, and pray for them which despitefully use you.

He sighed. *Jah*, that is what he *should* do. And he knew it. But that would be *so* difficult.

"*Gott,* I don't know if I can do that," He uttered the words under his breath.

I can do all things through Christ, which strengtheneth me.

"You would *have* to do it, Lord, because I can't. I have no good thoughts for this despicable Atlee person."

He finally hopped down from the buggy. Poor Blackie had probably been wondering what on earth he was doing, making him stand in front of the barn, yet not going in. "Sorry, buddy. We'll get you unhitched now so you can munch on some grass."

After taking care of the horse and putting up the carriage, he walked past the *dawdi haus* that had been vacant since Silas moved out and married Kayla. At one point in time, he'd asked to move in there himself. But *Mamm* had insisted they keep it available for married folk, and if he ever got around to taking a *fraa,* he could use it then. He was pretty sure that was *Mamm's* not-so-subtle way of telling him he should be settling down soon.

But he knew that when he did eventually settle with a bride, it likely wouldn't be on *Mamm* and *Dat's* farm. *Nee,* he wanted a place of his own like Silas and Kayla had. He couldn't imagine *Mamm* ramming her nose in, the way she had with Silas and Kayla. Silas had been ready to leave the *g'may* if need be to marry Kayla. And now that Paul had found someone he might consider settling down with, he completely understood where Silas had been coming from.

Love was a strange thing indeed, the way it caused people to do crazy things they'd never dreamed they would, and take risks with stakes higher than they'd thought worth it.

The moment he walked into the house, he heard the girls' muffled conversation. Martha and Amy must be sitting at the kitchen table. Good. Maybe he could escape upstairs unnoticed. He needed some time alone to pray. His mind had been way too *ferhoodled* lately, and connecting with *Der Herr* was a must.

He deposited his hat on the rack near the door and made what he hoped was a silent dash for the stairs.

"Paul!" Martha called.

So much for escaping unnoticed. "*Jah*?" he hollered from the stairs.

"*Kumm*. Amy is here to see you."

He groaned inwardly. Exactly what he didn't want. He wasn't ready to talk to her yet.

He turned around, attempted to place an amicable expression on his face, then entered the kitchen. "Hello, Amy."

"Where have you been?" Martha chastised. "You were supposed to be back hours ago."

"*Ach*. I was at Silas and Kayla's."

"Well, Amy's been waiting here for you. I told her you wouldn't be long."

Amy spoke up. "My *mamm* asked if you'd like to come for supper."

He took notice of her enthusiastic countenance and Silas's words slammed into his gut. *You know you are going to break her heart, right?* He sighed. *Ach.*

"I, uh, already have plans for supper tonight. Sorry." His hand troweled through his hair. It would be nice to take a shower prior to seeing Jenny tonight.

"You do?" Martha frowned. "Where? Since when?"

He wished his sister wasn't so nosy, especially with Amy here. "With Silas." Was all he answered.

"You can have supper with Silas any time. You should go with Amy." His sister insisted.

"They have company. And I gave my word." He shifted from one foot to the other.

"Company? What company?"

His gaze momentarily flicked toward Amy, then to the wooden floor. "Kayla's friend Sierra is visiting from California."

"What? This is the first I've heard of any such thing." Martha frowned.

Jennifer Spredemann

"It was a surprise visit." He explained.

Martha eyed her brother carefully. "How long is she staying?"

"I don't know. Probably a while." He glanced again at Amy, then at Martha. "I was actually hoping to speak with Amy. Alone."

"*Jah*. Okay." Martha finally took the hint.

Paul sighed in relief as his sister left the room. He turned back to Amy. "I'm sorry you've been waiting so long. I had no idea you were here. May I walk you to your buggy?"

"*Jah*." She stood from the table.

They walked toward the door and he placed his hat back on his head. "Tell your *mamm* thank you for the invitation."

"Maybe another time then?" Amy's voice sounded hopeful.

They stepped outside. "I, uh, actually, that's what I wanted to talk to you about." *Ach*, how did he say this without totally offending her?

He continued, "What I wanted to say is that I've decided to take a break from going to singings." He rushed on before he lost his nerve. "So I won't be giving you rides home anymore."

Confusion furrowed her forehead. "You're taking a break? I don't understand."

"I need time to figure some things out. You know

what I mean?"

"*Nee*. I don't."

"We've been *gut* friends, right?" He removed his hat, then placed it back on his head.

"*Jah...*" her tone conveyed uncertainty.

"And that's the thing." He swallowed. This was more difficult than he thought it would be. "I see you as a friend. *Only* a friend."

He'd seen the tears surface in her eyes before she abruptly looked away.

"*Ach*. I understand now. Goodbye, Paul." She made a hasty dash for the buggy.

Paul followed after her and handed the reins to her. "I'm sorry, Amy."

She nodded, backed up the carriage, and blew out of the driveway like her buggy wheels had caught fire.

Paul covered his eyes with his hand. *Ach*, he'd never meant to hurt her. He hated to admit it, but Silas had been right.

Martha jogged up to him as he made his way back to the house. "What happened? What did you say to her?"

"I'm not going to court her any longer."

"What?" Martha practically shouted. "Why?"

"*Ach*, calm down, *schweschder*."

"Don't tell me to calm down. You know Amy is

my best friend. How could you do that to her?"

"I only see her as a friend, Martha."

"What's wrong with you, Paul?" His sister frowned and fastened her arms across her chest.

"Nothing."

"Then why did you let a perfectly *gut* Amish woman go? She'd make *a gut fraa*."

"I'm sure she will. For someone else. Just not me."

She pointed a finger in his chest. "You like someone else, don't you?"

He shook his head. She was getting way too personal. "Who?"

"*Ach*, it's none of your beeswax, Martha. You're starting to sound like *Mamm*."

"Don't change the subject. Who did you dump Amy for? Megan Stoltzfus?"

"What? Megan Stoltzfus? *Nee*!"

"Then who?"

This must be the constant dripping the Bible talked about in Proverbs. "You don't know her."

"I don't..." His sister eyed him closely, examining his every twitch. "Wait! You don't have a thing for Kayla's *Englisch* friend, do you?"

He pressed his lips together.

"*Do you*, Paul?" Martha stomped her foot. "Tell me you *did not* just dump Amy for an *Englischer*."

"Okay, I won't tell you. You seem to have everything figured out already, so I don't need to say a word."

"Paul!"

"Who I court is none of your business."

"You're *courting* the *Englischer*?" Her pitch rose a notch.

"Like I said. None of your business. And don't go saying a word to *Mamm*, either." He pointed at her. "I mean it."

"Fine. But I'm going with you to Silas and Kayla's for supper."

"No, you are *not*. You weren't invited."

She snorted. "I don't need an invitation to visit my *bruder*."

"Sierra doesn't need a bunch of Amish folks coming to stare at her like she's an animal in the zoo." And he worried what people would assume if they noticed the bruise over her eye.

"Like you are?"

"We've already met. I'm a friend now." But, *jah*, he couldn't help but stare at her.

Martha rolled her eyes.

"Let her get comfortable and settled, then *maybe* you can meet her. I don't want her to get scared off."

"Comfortable and settled? How long is she staying for?"

Jennifer Spredemann

Hopefully forever? "I don't know."

EIGHT

The moment the clip-clop from Paul's horse met Jenny's ears, her heartrate increased rapidly. She glanced out the window near the sink to see if she could catch a glimpse of him as he drove toward the hitching post near the barn. She quickly finished washing up the last few dishes they'd used to prepare supper and placed them in the rack to dry. That way, there would be less dishes to wash after the meal.

She glanced down at her *Englisch* attire once again, nervous about how Paul would react. Would he like it? Would it turn him off because she now looked like an *Englischer*? And her hair. *Ach*, she wasn't used to wearing it down. It felt so foreign to her, especially since she'd had it styled. She did admit to herself, though, that she liked the way the makeup Kayla applied made her eyes stand out. Of course, she knew it was all vanity, but she might as well make the most out of the situation and enjoy it. At least, that's what Kayla had advised.

Which made her wonder...did Kayla miss the *Englisch* ways? She'd seemed so excited to help transform Amish Jenny into Sierra the *Englischer*, that Jenny couldn't help but get the feeling that she did. She couldn't imagine living *English* for twenty-plus years then joining a sect as strict as the Amish. There were just so many changes and adjustments one would have to make. But when Jenny had first come, she never would have guessed that Kayla had only been Amish for the last four-and-a-half years. She had apparently adjusted well to the culture.

"Sierra?" Kayla's oldest daughter, whom she'd met after their shopping excursion, had stepped into the kitchen.

"Yes, Bailey?"

"*Onkel* Paul and *Dat* want to talk to you outside." She bounced little Shiloh on her hip. "This *boppli* needs a snack." She pinched her nose with her fingers. "And a diaper change."

Jenny winked, happy the stench hadn't reached her own senses. "I think I'll leave you to that."

"Oh, *Mamm* said I shouldn't use Amish words around you unless I tell you what they are. *Boppli* means baby."

"Baby." She nodded. "Got it."

"I can teach you all you need to know if you want to become Amish."

Jenny suppressed a grin. "I appreciate that."

"I even know how to sew dresses now. And I made pants and a shirt for Judah." Bailey beamed.

Jenny thought of something *Englisch* to say. "I'm sure your mother is proud of you."

"We're not supposed to be proud, but I think she is too. *Dat* is even more proud, I think. But he isn't really my *dat*. I never met my first *dat*. He died before I was born." Bailey turned her head when the baby cried again. "I better go change Shiloh. And you should go see what *Dat* and Paul want."

A smiled tugged at Jenny's lips as she stepped from the kitchen into the living room. Time to see what Silas and Paul had called her for. She pushed the door open and momentarily bathed in the waning sunshine, lifting her face to the caress of the final rays of the day.

When she opened her eyes, she found Paul eying her, a spark of something akin to mischief in his eye.

"Wow, Je-Sierra! You look...amazing." His gaze roamed over her attire, hair, and face, several times as though he couldn't comprehend what his eyes were beholding.

She was sure and certain her face was all kinds of scarlet. "*Ach.*" She tugged at her shirt and glanced down at the strange-feeling trousers. "Do-do you think so?" She leaned close and whispered. "I feel weird."

"Well, you look awesome." He bent to her ear, his warm breath inciting another wave of palpitations. "And just like an *Englischer.*"

"Are you two finished flirting?" An amused grin lifted a corner of Silas's mouth.

Ach, Jenny hadn't seen Silas behind Paul. In fact, it seemed like she didn't notice much of anything when Paul was around.

"Never." Paul winked at her.

"Because we have matters that need to be discussed." Silas's brow lowered. "Let's walk to the barn in case any ears might be attempting to listen in the cornfield." He eyed the windows of the house.

"Sure." She followed the men to where the vehicle sat behind the barn.

"Paul and I fixed your tire. It seems like the fender might be bent a little, but looks like it will drive just fine."

"Oh, good." She blew out a breath. "Thank you."

"Have you contacted the owner?" Silas asked.

"*Ach,* I haven't been able to get ahold of him." She bit her bottom lip. "But maybe I can leave a message with my *mamm.*"

"Does she know where you are?"

"Nobody does. And I hope to keep it that way."

Paul frowned. "Because of Atlee?"

"Yes."

"We were thinking we could have a driver haul it back on a trailer," Silas interjected.

"That would be expensive, *ain't*-wouldn't it?

"Let us worry about that." Paul assured. "The most important thing is keeping you safe."

"*Denk*-thank you." She shook her head. "It's hard to become *Englisch* overnight."

"I can imagine." Paul offered an encouraging smile. "And it hasn't even been a night yet."

"I'll try to get ahold of someone, then." She looked at Silas. "When do you think they can take the car back?"

"Probably as soon as you say the word. This week for sure."

"Okay. I'll call right now." Her insides trembled at the thought of speaking with anyone back home. She pictured Atlee listening in on the conversation, furiously jotting down every detail. She needed to be careful not to say too much or give her location away.

The safest place to call would probably be the bakery. Either *Mamm* or one of her sisters would answer the phone. Hopefully, they stayed after closing hours today. Otherwise, she'd have to try again another day.

"Do you want me to come with you?" Paul offered.

"No, that's not necessary. But thanks for offering." She smiled. "I shouldn't be long."

Paul nodded, but she could see the disappointment in his gaze.

She rushed toward the shanty, wanting to hurry up and make the call, yet dreading it at the same time.

She dialed the number to her family's bakery and silently prayed *Mamm* would be the one to answer the phone. Her heart pounded with each ring and she nearly hung up after the third ring, but someone picked up on the other end.

"Christner's Bakery, what may I get for you?"

"Who...is this?"

A gasp sounded on the other end. "Jenny? Is that you? We've been worried sick about you."

"I'm fine, *Mamm*. I'm safe."

"Atlee has come by the house and the bakery several times a day looking for you."

Ach, she didn't want to think about Atlee. "Will you please tell Mr. Sanderson that I'll get his car back to him as soon as possible?"

"You were lucky he didn't call the police. I assured him that you would return it."

"*Denki. Jah*, I will have it back to him this week."

"Oh, good. You're coming home, then?"

"*Nee*. I cannot come home." Her voice trembled, but she stayed the course. "*Mamm*...Atlee...he's not how you think he is. He wasn't *gut* to me."

"What do you mean, *dochder*?"

"I tried to tell you before. That's why I had to get away." She sobbed. "He...he hurt me."

"What are you talking about, Jenny? Atlee, *our* Atlee, the minister's *sohn*?"

"Yes. Remember my eye, it wasn't a rake that did that. That's what Atlee wanted me to tell people. He threatened to hurt me if I didn't."

"Jenny..." The doubt in her mother's tone was unmistakable. "That boy loves you. You should see him right now. He's in a bad way."

"You don't believe me? He doesn't love me! He hurt me, *Mamm*." She tried to keep back another sob. "I-I have to go."

She slammed the phone's receiver back into its cradle, unable to keep from breaking down.

It wasn't right. Why did everybody take Atlee's word over hers? He was the minister's son, *jah*, but hadn't her swollen eye been evidence enough? Of course, Atlee had insisted on going into the house with her afterward and finding an ice pack, pretending to care, especially when others were around. He'd even joked about her clumsiness, saying it was a good thing she had him to look after her. She'd always felt two inches tall when he'd craft tales about her. And everyone *believed* him—that was the worst part about it.

She hated him for it—for all of it. He should have gone to Hollywood for a career in acting. Surely he would have received one of those fancy awards that the magazines in the Walmart checkout line were always boasting about.

But the people *here* were different. They didn't even know her, yet they *believed* her. Kayla believed her, Silas believed her, and Paul believed her—enough to help her change her identity. Enough to give her a place to stay, food to eat, a job, friendship, and so much more. They didn't owe her anything. She was a virtual stranger to them. She didn't deserve their kindness, but she certainly appreciated it.

She forced her tears away and dried her face before stepping out of the phone shanty. No need for anyone to see her distraught. She didn't need to burden these good people with her problems. They'd already done so much for her. She wished there was something she could do to return the favor.

A lantern suddenly flicked to life inside her head.

Ach, that was what she would do to show her appreciation! She would make a special treat for them—something fancy she'd made at the bakery back home. She wished she knew what their favorite flavors were. She'd hate to make something with, say, coconut only to discover that they hate coconut. She'd have to make more than one dessert just in case. Too bad she hadn't thought of the idea sooner or else she could have picked up the ingredients when she and Kayla had been in town earlier.

Maybe she'd inquire of their favorite flavors in a roundabout sort of way. She could instigate a casual conversation with Bailey. The girl seemed to love volunteering information.

Paul waited as patiently as he could for Jenny to finish up her phone call. He imagined it might be quite stressful for her, especially if she was speaking with her mother for the first time since she'd been gone. He suddenly realized that, other than the situation with Atlee, he knew precious little about Jenny and where she'd come from. But he hoped to change that soon. He'd be over the moon if he could talk her into a buggy ride tonight.

He'd just finished brushing down Blackie, as Jenny

approached the house. "Were you able to get ahold of someone?"

"*Jah*, my...I mean, yes, my mother."

"Good." He shifted from one foot to the other, then gestured toward the porch swing. "Would you like to sit? Kayla said it would be a few minutes yet until supper is ready."

She hesitated. "I should probably help her."

"Everything's all taken care of." He'd made sure of that, offering to set the table while Jenny had been on the phone, so that they'd be able to talk a few moments.

"Okay, then." She followed him to the swing and sat down.

He glanced in her direction. "How did your conversation go? Was your mother worried?"

"It went okay. I told her someone would drop off Mr. Sanderson's car. She said he didn't call the police."

He blew out a breath. "Well, that in itself is a relief, and good news."

"For sure. I'm thankful for that." She nodded. "My mother did seem worried, but I told her that I was safe."

"That's good." He set the swing into motion with the toe of his boot. "Do you mind?"

"No. This breeze feels nice." She lifted her face and

indulged in the fresh stream of air.

"It does. Would you..." He swallowed, his hands suddenly clammy. "Would you like to go for a ride after supper?"

She tugged in her bottom lip between her teeth, a habit he found attractive. "Paul, I like you. But I don't know if I'm ready for a relationship yet. Do you know what I mean?"

"Certainly." He swallowed his disappointment. He should have known it wouldn't be that easy. "Is friendship acceptable then?"

"Of course."

"Then...how about just a walk after supper? As friends? I realized that I don't know much about you, but I would like to learn."

She pressed her lips together, seeming to contemplate his question. "Sure. Why not?"

"Wonderful." He smiled easily. He turned at the sound of footsteps. "I think supper might be ready now."

"Good, because I'm famished."

NINE

"Is everyone ready to eat?" Silas stood by the table singling out his brother.

"You know I'm *always* ready to eat!" Paul winked at the *kinner*. He made his way to the table and Jenny followed suit.

"Can Sierra sit next to me?" Bailey pleaded.

"If she wants to." Kayla smiled. "Sierra?"

She nodded. "I'd love to, Bailey."

Jenny watched as each person took their place— Silas sat at the head of the table with Kayla to his left and little Judah to his right, in a booster seat on top of the wooden bench. Between Kayla and Silas, there was a highchair occupied by little Shiloh. Bailey sat on Kayla's other side, and Jenny sat next to Bailey. Paul sat across from Bailey, next to his nephew, Judah.

They all bowed their heads for the silent prayer. As soon as they did, Bailey turned to Jenny. "How long are you going to be staying with us?"

"I don't know yet." She smiled at the girl.

"Will you become Amish too, like me and *Mamm* did?"

She glanced up at the other adults, who were filling their plates. "I don't know." She took a drink of her water.

"*Ach*, I have an idea! A *wunderbaar* idea! You can become Amish like me and *Mamm*, and marry *Onkel* Paul, like *Mamm* did *Dat*!"

Jenny nearly spewed her water out of her mouth, but instead began choking on it. She was certain her face must have erupted in flames.

"Bailey, that's enough," Silas said. "Not too many questions. Let Sierra eat her supper."

"I still say it's a *wunderbaar* idea," Bailey insisted.

Jenny was too embarrassed to make eye contact with Paul.

Bailey then leaned back and looked under the table. "*Onkel* Paul, why is your foot rubbing against mine?"

"*Ach*, I, uh, sorry. I thought it was...never mind." Now it was Paul's turn to don a crimson hue.

Jenny pressed her lips together to hold in a chuckle, then she glanced up at Silas and Kayla, who both burst into laughter. Jenny couldn't help but join in.

"I...uh...need to..." Paul abruptly shot up from the

table, and disappeared down the hall.

That sent Silas into a hooting fit, eyes filling up with tears and spilling over onto his cheeks and beard.

Not wanting to be left out, Bailey giggled too. "What are you all laughing about? What's so funny, *Mamm*?"

Even the little ones were giggling now and little Shiloh was clapping her hands together.

Another round of merriment erupted, until Jenny's stomach clenched in pain and she suppressed a groan. She wiped away her own tears. When was the last time she'd shared such hilarious moments with anyone? Had she *ever*?

After a few calming breaths, she was able to resume filling her plate. When the excitement died down, Paul eventually reemerged, head down.

They all held back the urge to burst into another fit of laughter. Jenny couldn't lift her head to look at Paul. And even if she could, she was certain Paul was too embarrassed to lift his head to meet her eyes. Poor thing. He stared steadfastly at his plate, shoveling food into his mouth.

A sense of normalcy returned to the table and everyone resumed passing food, dishing it onto their plates, and eating. An occasional comment was made by one of the *kinner*, but other than that, the remainder of the meal was mostly silent.

Jenny liked this family a lot. Her father had never tolerated much talking, and certainly not laughing, at the table. Was this family different because Kayla had been an *Englischer*? Or had Silas and Paul been raised in a similar manner? Either way, she found herself drawn to this family even more. They possessed something she didn't, and she desperately craved whatever it was she was missing.

Jenny offered to wash dishes after the meal, but Kayla shooed her and Paul off once she'd been informed of their plans to take a walk. Truthfully, Paul had hoped to break the ice after dinner by joining Jenny at the sink. The dinner situation had just been awkward.

They walked away from the house, but stayed on Silas and Kayla's property. Someday, Paul hoped to have a place of his own. But this, like marriage, wasn't something he'd been seriously considering—until he'd met Jenny. How was it that she had this effect on him? Had him thinking on these things? It made absolutely no logical sense.

"I'm sorry for embarrassing you at supper." Paul shook his head and sighed. "I don't know *what* I was thinking."

Jenny giggled. "*Ach*, I can't remember the last time I laughed so much."

"I'm glad I can at least provide amusement for you."

"It's...okay. But I don't think I'll ever forget it." She smiled, bumping his shoulder on purpose.

"And I don't think I'll *ever* be able to live it down. That right there is blackmail material for Silas."

She laughed. "Have you two always been this way?"

"Pretty much." He smiled.

"It's nice that you get along so well."

"Do you not get along with your siblings?" He frowned. "How many brothers and sisters do you have, anyway?"

"We get along okay, I guess. But it's not the same as you and Silas. I think you two have a special relationship." She shrugged. "I have two sisters and two brothers. I'm the youngest of the bunch. How about you?"

"There are six of us. I have three younger sisters, and two brothers—one older, one younger."

"So you're second in line, then."

He nodded. "I'm wondering something."

"What's that?"

"If you don't mind telling me, how did you get

mixed up with this Atlee character?"

She shrugged. "His father is one of the favorite ministers in our community. He speaks messages that are meaningful, you know? His family is wonderful. They are all very kind and caring. I thought *that* was what I was getting into with Atlee, but it just wasn't so. So for others to believe that one of the family is not that way—especially when he appears to be in *their* presence—is nearly impossible. *I* probably wouldn't have believed it, if I hadn't experienced it firsthand."

"That's a shame. Was he always like that and you just didn't see it then?"

"I don't know. I don't think so. It started out with little things, you know, like him grabbing my arm and squeezing a little too tightly."

"And that didn't shoot off warnings in your head?"

"It did. But then he would apologize. At first, I thought he was sincere, that he really didn't mean to do it. He was very...affectionate. It is difficult when your heart and your emotions are wrapped up in everything. It just complicates things."

"*Jah.*" Paul frowned. "Did you ever think to go to the leaders?"

"No, I could never do that."

"Why not?"

"Well, first of all, they might think I am making things up. Especially if Atlee claimed I was lying to them, which is what would happen. Second, even if they did believe me, it wouldn't change Atlee. It likely would have made him worse."

"So...okay, I don't understand." He shook his head. "Why would you stay in a relationship with a person like that?"

"By the time I realized how bad he was, we were both invested in the relationship. He wouldn't let me leave. Really, there was no place I could go to get away from him. I saw him at meeting. He knew where I lived. He knew where I worked. And the one time I mentioned breaking things off, he became very upset and he threatened me. I didn't know what to do."

Paul squeezed his eyes closed, attempting to cool his temper. "Is that how you ended up here?"

"Basically."

A thought dawned on him. "Do you think maybe he was using drugs? I've heard that can change someone's personality, make them more aggressive."

She frowned. "I guess it's possible, but I've never seen him use any."

"What are you going to do now? Do you think you might want to settle here?" *Please say yes.*

"*Ach,* I'd like to attend church to see how it is.

Learn what the *Ordnung* says and how it differs from ours back home." She shrugged. "Maybe eventually." She looked down at her clothes. "But I'm *Englisch* now. I don't know how that would work."

"Well, I'm sure that Bailey would be more than willing to teach you Amish." He winked and smiled.

Jenny laughed. "As a matter of fact, she's already offered."

"Oh." He snapped his fingers. "Wait a minute. I have an idea. At least, I *think* I might."

Jenny giggled again. He really liked hearing that sound. "What is it?"

"Have you thought about changing your name? I mean, legally speaking? Because if you could join the church as an *Englischer*, with an *Englisch* name, your Amish name would never be known. You wouldn't have to worry about Atlee finding out—or anyone from your home district—because you would actually *be* Sierra."

She frowned and shook her head. "I don't know. I feel so bad about all of this already. Have you considered what might happen if we were found out? Wouldn't you and Silas and Kayla be put in the *Bann* for going along with all of this? I hate that I am putting you all in a situation where you have to lie to your friends and loved ones. How is Bailey going to feel when she realizes everyone's lied to her? How is she going to trust her parents again? I'm responsible for all this deception. It just feels wrong. Honestly, I think it might be better if I just leave."

His heartrate accelerated. She couldn't leave. Just thinking about her out there all alone... He'd go crazy if he didn't know where she was or whether she was safe or not. *Nee*, he had to convince her otherwise. "And go where?"

"I don't know."

He reached over and brushed her hand with his fingers. "Jenny, they will understand when and if they learn the truth. And a little bit of discomfort on our part is worth it if we can keep you safe. I honestly feel like *Der Herr* brought you here."

"For what reason?"

A fraa for me? He didn't understand how all of a sudden he craved a wife. He'd been perfectly content as a bachelor up until he met Jenny. "Perhaps that is to be determined."

He continued to reason. "But think of it this way. The leaders will not need to seek out your past if they believe you are an *Englischer*. They will not need a letter from your bishop saying that you are in good standing, and they won't need to know where you're from or who your family is. None of that will matter if you are coming out of the *Englisch* world. You will not have to worry about your family finding out because it would be the *Englisch* Sierra that is joining the *g'may* and not Amish Jenny. And Atlee will have no way of finding you."

"*Ach*, it does sound tempting."

"And then maybe years down the road, after you find out that Atlee has moved on and married, it might be safe to visit your folks. I would be willing to go with you." *Hopefully as your husband.*

A deep frown settled on her face.

"What's wrong?"

"I just...I hate to think of Atlee married to someone else and her having to go through everything I have. And to be settled with him. Do you know what I mean?"

"*Jah*, I can understand that. But you really don't have any control over that situation."

"I would just feel bad, maybe I should try to warn the person."

"Like I said, that's a situation you can't control. And if your own family didn't believe you..."

"*Ach*, I guess you have a point."

"You can always pray about it. Who knows? Maybe *Der Herr* will step in and change him."

"Do you think it's possible?"

He nodded, then looked into her eyes. "Please. Stay here. With us. Make a new life for yourself here."

She appeared as though she were considering the idea. "Could we maybe discuss this with Silas and Kayla to see what they say?"

"*Jah*, of course. We will pray about it too, that *Der Herr* will direct your steps according to His will."

"I would feel silly asking *Der Herr* to bless deception."

"You can't think of it like that. We have no ill intent here, only to keep you from harm."

"*Jah*, okay. I guess you're right."

"So, do you like it here so far?"

"*Ach*, I love it. Your family is wonderful."

He chuckled. "You haven't met them all yet. You might just change your mind."

"For real?"

He shrugged. "My *mamm* can be pretty overbearing at times. You should have seen when Kayla and Bailey first came. Once she found out that Silas was interested in an *Englischer*..." He shook his head and whistled. "Let's just say she was *not* pleased."

"So, does she not like Kayla then?"

"She's okay with her now, I think. But they've never been close." He shrugged. "Maybe Silas went about it the wrong way, I don't know."

"What do you mean?"

"Uh..." He rubbed the back of his neck. "Kayla and Silas sort of spent a couple of nights alone together in the house they now live in...*before* they were married."

Her eyebrows shot up. "Oh."

"Nothing happened. It was all pretty innocent, but my *mamm* flew off the handle."

"I can imagine. That's not...and for an Amish man and an *Englisch* woman..."

"Yep. Pretty scandalous stuff." He shook his head. "And then the whole thing with Bailey..."

"Bailey?"

"Kayla's daughter, born out-of-wedlock. She's actually the daughter of Silas's best friend, who died before she was born."

"Oh, that's sad."

"*Jah*, but *Der Herr* brought them here and worked it all out."

She nodded. "Kayla had mentioned something about that."

"Anyway, enough about all that." He studied her carefully. "I never asked. How old are you?"

"I'm twenty. You?"

"Twenty-two."

"What do you do? Like for a job?"

"I was or am a farrier, a smithy, for the most part.

Then Silas and I kind of started a business." He shrugged.

"What kind of business?"

"We forge things out of metal. Would you like to see?"

"I'd love to."

TEN

After Paul turned on a propane lamp that hung from the ceiling, Jenny surveyed the contents of the large pole barn's interior. Metal workings of all kinds lined the walls. Some things, like wrought iron plant shelves, stood on their own, while smaller items filled the wooden shelves. Several hanging metal windchimes of various sizes called her attention when a gust of wind picked up and blew through the shop.

Paul quickly closed the barn door behind them. "*Ach*, we can't have the dust getting in here. That makes a lot more work."

"Oh my goodness, Paul! You and Silas made all of this?" She walked over to one of the windchimes. "These are beautiful."

"Do you like them?" He shifted from one foot to the other. It was a habit Jenny had noticed, something Paul did when he was nervous or unsure.

She lightly touched his arm to reassure him. "You guys do great work." She picked up one of the metal signs which boasted a popular Bible verse. "Are these allowed in your homes here?"

"*Jah.*" He blew out a breath and relaxed his stance.

"I've always loved windchimes. The sound is so peaceful and calming, isn't it?"

He nodded. "I like them too."

"Do you sell many?"

"Some. When an occasional *Englischer* comes by or if one of the Plain folk wants to get something special for a gift." He shrugged. "They're a little expensive so we don't sell a ton of them. The smaller, cheaper items are what sell best."

"Where all do you sell them?"

"We have some in Silas's store. A few of the other stores around carry them as well."

"I bet these would sell really well in Holmes County. Lots of tourists go through there."

"You think?"

"Yes, for sure. Do you make anything with a horse and buggy? Smaller things, like keychains and such?"

He moved to a shelf on the opposite side of the shop and reached into a plastic basket. "Like this?"

She moved to see what he held in his hand. She examined the black metal buggy keychain. "Yes.

Perfect. What do you usually sell these for?"

"A couple of dollars."

"You could get five for it in a tourist place."

His lips twisted. "I don't know if it's worth that much."

She smiled. "Not to you, but tourists will pay that all day long. And if they know it was made by someone who is Amish, they are happy to do it, because they know they are supporting your livelihood."

He walked back over to the windchimes and gently moved his hand over one to produce a light clanging sound. "Do you have a favorite?"

"I don't know if I could choose. They all have their own unique sound." She tapped one of the chimes with her finger to set it into motion. "They're all lovely."

"I'd like to give you one. If you want."

She shook her head, but gratefulness filled her heart. "Paul, it's too much. I appreciate it, but..."

"*Nee*, it's not too much. Please, choose whichever one you want. I mean it. It will...be something to remember me by." His brow lowered as though the words caused him physical pain.

She was quite certain she wouldn't *ever* be forgetting Paul Miller. *Those kind eyes.*

"But if you insist." She touched his arm and their

gazes met. Something flashed in his eyes. Admiration? Respect, maybe? *Love? Nee,* it couldn't be.

She'd seen reflections in Atlee's eyes before too—sometimes desire, usually rage. But never whatever it was she was seeing in Paul's gaze.

He waited patiently as her fingers glided over each one, the walls of the shop reverberating with the lovely clanging sounds. *Ach*, it was so difficult to choose a favorite. "I think maybe this one."

"You're sure?"

She moved her fingers across the pipes again. "*Jah.*"

"Good choice." He grinned, removing the wind chime from its hook. "I named this one 'church bells' because that's what the sound reminds me of."

She swallowed, loving the pleasure reflecting in his eyes. What a *wunderbaar* gift. The gesture seemed intimate somehow. Like he was offering her piece of his soul. Was she reading too much into it? "*Denki*, Paul."

He cleared his throat. "Thank you," he said, gently reminding her that she was now *Englisch*.

"Yes, thank you," she corrected herself. She had to remember that she could no longer use Amish words, if she was going to be believable. If only the clothes on the outside could transform the inside. But...she didn't *want* to be an *Englischer*. She loved the Amish ways—well, most of them anyhow. She didn't want to lose or forget her Amish heritage.

"It's only temporary." Had Paul read her mind? "I know this is hard for you, Jenny. I'm sorry."

"How do you do that?"

"What?"

"How do you know me so well?"

He shrugged. "I don't know. I guess I can just sense it. I see that you're conflicted. You're worried, a little fearful, maybe. I wish there was something I could do for you."

Jenny couldn't stop her chin from quivering, or the tears that formed in her eyes, at his tender words.

"*Ach*, shh..." His brow lowered and he held out a hand toward her. "*Kumm*."

She surrendered, allowing him to pull her into his outstretched arms. She couldn't keep back a sob as her head rested against his chest. This was the first time she'd broken down since she'd left everything behind and fled for her safety, and possibly her life. The fear, uncertainty, and pain of the past couple of days seemed to release as the tears continued to roll down her cheeks.

Paul's hand rubbed her back in a soothing motion and she inhaled his masculine scent—she wasn't sure if it was soap or cologne of some sort—but it was intoxicating nonetheless. His lips pressed to the top of her head as he murmured gently to her.

Ach, Paul Miller was a dream—too *gut* to be true, really. Essentially the exact opposite of Atlee. Which meant Paul happened to be precisely what she needed, what she craved.

He pulled back a moment and she attempted to read his features. His gaze strayed to her lips, then back to her eyes. He stepped away, but took her hands in his. "May I...pray with you?"

Pray? Ach, not exactly what she had in mind. She nodded and bowed her head, anyhow.

"*Gott*, You know Jenny's situation and what is in her heart. Please be with her and bring her comfort. Keep her safe in Your arms, and guide her steps. Amen."

Her eyes burst open at his audible words. "You...pray out loud?"

He released her hands, to her disappointment.

He chuckled. "*Nee*, not usually. I've heard Silas do it a time or two. He said that sometimes he feels the Spirit leading him to. That was my first time."

"Did you feel the Spirit leading you?"

"I believe I did. I think you needed to hear the words, maybe?"

"*Jah*. Yes. You never really know what folks are

praying or *if* they are praying when it is silent. Of course, they are praying to God, not me, so I don't really need to know. But I liked hearing your prayer for me. It was nice."

"Should we go inside now? They're probably wondering where we are."

She could've stayed out here with Paul all night. "Sure."

She began following him, then stopped. "Paul?"

He turned around to look at her.

She swallowed. "Thank you. For everything." The words didn't seem enough to express the gratitude she felt in her heart. Truthfully, she'd never had a friend like Paul, and she was truly grateful for his friendship.

He nodded. "My pleasure."

Paul flicked the reins a little more aggressively than he should have. "Sorry, Blackie."

What on earth had he been thinking? Jenny specifically stated that she was *not* interested in a relationship. She wanted to be friends. Just friends. Only friends.

So why did he have to go and pull her into his arms like that? *Ach,* he'd almost kissed her! It would have been a disastrous move. She probably would have shot out of that barn and never spoken to him again.

And then the windchime. They weren't even courting and he'd offered her a windchime! Something that might be a special gift for someone you're engaged or married to.

He could not believe how close he'd come to blowing it.

And that was exactly why he hadn't stuck around for dessert. He hadn't stayed for games. Nothing. Because if he had, and then Jenny walked out with him to say goodnight...he just couldn't.

ELEVEN

*J*enny startled and shot up out of bed at the loud noise. Was Atlee here? Had he found out where she was? *Nee*, he couldn't be. It was just her imagination, wasn't it?

She tiptoed to the bedroom door and peeked through the crack, but saw nothing. She turned her head and pressed her ear to the door. Nothing but Kayla stirring in the kitchen.

Ach, had she imagined the whole thing? She took a deep breath and her heartbeat slowed to normal.

What time was it anyway?

She began to move away from the door, but not before hearing two male voices. Silas and Paul.

Paul. She closed her eyes, recalling the dream she'd so rudely been awakened from. It had been a continuation from the evening before. But instead of Paul leaving the shop after praying with her, he had lowered his head to meet her lips. She'd reveled in the feel of his soft lips on hers. He hadn't been clumsy at all, like he knew what he was doing. His hand had moved to the back of her head and entangled in her hair as their passion intensified. She'd tilted her head slightly and he'd deepened the kiss, pulling her taut against his body, sending waves of desire through her.

And then...*jah,* maybe it was a good thing she'd been awakened suddenly. She didn't need to continue that dream. Perhaps it had been *Der Herr* who had woken her up.

But she didn't think she'd *ever* forget those kisses— the vivid moments of passion that had only happened in her imagination. And *that* was a crying shame.

Ach, if Atlee ever knew she was dreaming about Paul, she'd be fearing for Paul's safety. The one time he'd seen her merely glance at good-looking man, he'd flown off the handle. He hadn't liked her working at her folks' bakery, either, because she'd occasionally have contact with male customers. Whenever she saw him coming into the bakery, she made sure to let one of her sisters run the front counter. She couldn't chance him threatening one of their customers.

She didn't even want to entertain thoughts of what Atlee had been doing since she'd skipped town. He had to be irate. *Mamm* had said that he'd been around persistently. She wondered how long it would take him to forget about her, or at least give up his pursuit of her.

She couldn't think of Atlee now. *Nee*, she needed to get dressed and start her day.

She sighed and walked to the small closet. *Ach*, no Amish dresses! They'd been folded and put away in her suitcase. In her dreamy state, she'd completely forgotten. She could no longer be Plain. This would certainly take some getting used to.

"Okay, Sierra. Time to don your threads." She laughed at herself. That was something that Kayla had said that Jenny thought sounded absolutely ridiculous. Especially coming from the mouth of an Amish woman. What did it even mean anyway? She was pretty certain it was something Kayla had uttered in jest, but without knowing the culture or the meaning behind it, it had been totally lost on her. Kayla eventually explained that it meant to put your clothes on. So now, she joked about it to herself.

But joking aside, she *did* need to get dressed. When they'd been shopping, it felt like she'd purchased a ton of *Englisch* clothes; but looking at the selection now, they hadn't really purchased all that much. She opted for a pair of trousers that fit a little looser than the ones she'd worn yesterday. *Nee*, not trousers, jeans

Kayla had insisted she call them. But they still looked like men's trousers to her. And she chose the orange top Kayla insisted was "adorable" on her.

She certainly gave Kayla points for encouragement and enthusiasm. Too bad it didn't make Jenny feel any more *Englisch* than what she was. She didn't want to be *Englisch*, though.

She hurriedly dressed and ran a quick brush through her hair. She began absentmindedly twisting her hair into a bun, and then suddenly dropped it when she remembered she wasn't supposed to wear it up like an Amish woman. Not that she'd never worn it down at home. But that had usually been after a bath when allowing her hair to dry, and with only her family around. But never around others who weren't family. And to not wear a prayer *kapp. Ach.* She felt naked without a proper covering.

When she'd made it to the kitchen, Paul was setting his empty coffee cup next to the sink. He looked up, caught her eye, and lifted an easy smile, which she returned.

Kayla stood near the stove. "I kept breakfast hot for you, if you'd like some. The men always start early in the shop, then Silas readies the pony cart for Bailey to drive to school."

Jenny turned to Kayla. "Has she left for school?"

"*Jah*. About twenty minutes ago, sleepyhead."
Paul winked. "Must've been some dream." He lifted a
knowing brow.

Her face felt hot again. There's no way on earth he
could know what she'd dreamt. *Jah, it certainly was!*
If he only knew. She'd be swallowed up in
embarrassment for sure and certain.

"Wishful thinking, huh?" Silas laughed and
slapped his brother on the back. He turned to Jenny.
"Kayla can show you the store today and get you
started in there if you'd like."

"That would be great." Any type of work would be
wunderbaar, but she wondered what she had need of
money for. Because she was quite certain that Silas
wouldn't allow her to contribute to the family's
income. She could use it to buy ingredients for baked
goods, though. Perhaps that was how she could bless
this family, who had shown her nothing but kindness
and friendship.

After Silas and Paul stepped outside, Jenny sat
down to eat. Kayla joined her at the table with a cup
of something steaming.

"Did you sleep alright?"

"*Wunderbaar.*"

"Wonderful." Kayla corrected. "Just remember if
you slip around Bailey, it's okay. She'll assume that

you're learning a few Amish words and she'll probably try to teach you more. But if Plain folks come into the store, you'll have to be careful."

"Yes. And I'm trying to train myself to lose my accent. It's difficult. I honestly don't know if I can pull this off."

"Well, if I'm there with you, just let me do the talking. You don't have to speak much, and when you have to talk, concentrate on your speech."

"Okay."

Kayla shook her head and smiled.

"What?"

"Paul." Her grin widened and she rolled her eyes. "He has it bad for you. I've never seen him this way about a girl before. He doesn't know what to do with himself, poor thing." She laughed. "And Silas can't seem to stop teasing him."

"Paul said he teased Silas about you when you two first met."

"He sure did. I guess this is payback time."

"That's...I love it. The fact that they are not overly serious with each other. And they seem really close." She dug into her scrambled eggs.

"They're several years apart. Eight years, actually. Since Silas is the oldest child, I think he feels like he has to protect his younger brothers and sisters. Silas said when he was younger, Paul was like his shadow. Even when he married his first wife, he just lived in the *dawdi haus* next door to his parents' place. When Silas considered leaving the Amish to marry me, Paul all but broke down. They certainly love each other."

"Silas was going to leave the Amish?"

"If that was the only way we could marry, then yes. But God worked out a way for us."

"I don't understand, sometimes."

"What do you mean?"

She shrugged. "God."

"Well, first of all, I think that if we *could* fully understand God, then He wouldn't be God. His ways are past finding out."

"Why do you suppose some people have an easy life, while others struggle so much?"

"Wow, that's a loaded question." Kayla eyed her. "Do you think *my* life is easy?"

Jenny shrugged.

"Trust me, it's been anything but. Don't get me wrong, I'm very grateful for the life God has blessed me with, but it is far from easy."

"Do you struggle? Like with being Amish?"

"Honestly, yes, sometimes. I was used to basically doing whatever I wanted. Now, there are a list of strict rules I have to live by. So, yes, occasionally I do struggle. But then I see Silas and our children and the blessing that they are, and it's totally worth it."

"I wonder sometimes...about Atlee. When I first began a relationship with him, he seemed normal. But then, he just changed. He became someone I didn't recognize. And then, he turned possessive and mean and angry. And I'm the one who suffered because of it. I was innocent in all of it." She wiped away a tear. "I just wonder why God didn't prevent him from hurting me. Why doesn't God stop people like that?"

"The best answer I can offer is free will. Love can only exist when there is free will. It has to be a conscious choice. Just like Atlee cannot force you to love him, and you cannot force him to love you. God does not force His love or His will on any of us. We choose whether to follow Him or not. He did His part. He made a choice for love when Jesus sacrificed Himself and shed His blood on the cross."

"I don't understand what that has to do with my situation."

"*Ach*, I don't think I'm explaining it the right way. But with free will, we also have the opportunity to do evil. And I think evil happens when we don't trust God. Do you remember in the book of Joshua, where God says that He set life and death and blessing or cursing before the children of Israel? It was their choice to follow God or no. It is the same for every person."

"But can't He just stop the evil, the tragedies?"

"I've asked the same questions. Why did my parents both have to die at such a young age? But then, I see the other side of it. If my parents hadn't passed away, I would have never met Silas. I wouldn't have my beautiful babies."

Jenny nodded.

"God is sovereign. He knows what is up ahead for us. And He promises that all things work together for the good for those who love Him and are called according to His purpose. We just have to place our faith in Him and know that He knows what's best." Kayla shrugged. "He brought you *here*, right?"

"Yes." She frowned.

"I don't know, but maybe you're here for a reason too. I don't think you and Paul narrowly escaping an accident was a coincidence. You were on that same road, at that same time. And you needed help. I'm not God, so I don't know, but maybe all that happened because you and Paul were supposed to meet. Or maybe because you and I were supposed to meet."

"Do you think I'm supposed to become an *Englischer*?"

"I can't say. But maybe temporarily."

"Paul suggested I change my name legally. *Really* become Sierra. He reasoned that if I did, I could attend the *g'may* as an *Englischer*, and then convert as an *Englischer*. Atlee wouldn't know anything about it because Jenny Christner wouldn't exist anymore. I wouldn't have to worry about my name being published anywhere. I could very easily become Amish because, well, I am. I would just have a different name."

"And how do you feel about that?"

"Conflicted. Confused. I used to think I knew exactly what right and wrong were. But now, I'm all *ferhoodled*."

"That's definitely a word you don't want to use as an *Englischer*." Kayla laughed. "I can kind of understand. It wasn't easy for me to become Amish. At least you already know the language. I don't know. It's really something that you will have to decide."

"I just...I hate the dishonesty. And I feel like I'm not trusting God. I mean, He can keep me safe, right?"

"He can. Yet, you came here because you weren't safe. You are hiding out like Joshua and Caleb in the Bible. Maybe this is God's way of keeping you safe, just like He kept the spies safe."

"I guess I never really thought of it that way."

"Whatever you decide to do, we will support you. But I think you should know that this community does not readily accept *Englischers* into the *g'may*."

"*Ach*, really? I didn't realize that. And I'm already a baptized member of my community, in good standing. At least, I was before I left. It would be weird to do it all again."

"And you said that Atlee's father is a minister, right? He'd for sure find out that you're here. So transferring easily is not really an option for you."

"I know." She frowned.

"Well, it's something to pray about. Personally, I don't think Paul's suggestion is necessarily a bad one." Kayla glanced down at Jenny's food. "Well, I should probably quit talking your ear off and let you finish eating. Your breakfast is probably cold by now. Besides, I think I heard the babies stirring. They're late risers today. I need to feed them and get them ready for the day."

"I can help." Jenny smiled. She'd always loved little ones. "And then we can go to the store."

TWELVE

Jenny followed Kayla and her small children through the entrance of the small store. It sat at the end of their driveway and, if it hadn't been for the sign, Jenny would have assumed it was just an out building. She guessed they probably didn't get a whole lot of customers, and wondered if they advertised anywhere.

She smiled when she noticed a few of Paul's windchimes hanging inside. She moved to touch one, causing a rich mournful sound to clang through the air.

"We keep those inside in the evening, but usually take them out during the day. They just go on those hooks on the front porch there." Kayla pointed outside. "We alternate the windchimes with the hanging flower pots."

"Would you like me to move the windchimes now?"

"Sure. You can do that."

Jenny attempted to recall her dream as she placed each chime on its hook. She loved the sounds each one made. She was certain she'd cherish Paul's gift as long as she lived. She hurried back inside to help Kayla.

Kayla held little Shiloh on her hip, but kept ahold of Judah's hand.

"I bet it's hard running this store with the little ones."

"It is, which is why I'm grateful to have you here. Silas and Paul help out once in a while, but for the most part, it's me and the *kinner*. I have a playpen in the back if I need to set them down, so that's helpful. But they tend to get antsy cooped up in here. There's no place for them to run around."

"Poor babies." She stuck out a pouty lip as she tweaked Shiloh's plump cheek.

"Bailey's a big help, but she's gone most of the day."

"Are you open every day?" She guessed not, since the store had been closed yesterday when she'd arrived.

"*Nee*. But maybe with you helping out here, we can expand our hours."

Jenny nodded, then surveyed the outline of the store. "Have you thought of having a little bakery in here?" she suggested.

"*Ach*, not really. I'm too busy with the *kinner* and such to keep up with that. I do make a few things that we sell. My pot pie is pretty popular with our customers."

"Well, I could help if you want to set up a bakery. I love to bake." Jenny smiled. She eyed the empty glass cases near the side wall. "This would be perfect. It looks like you're already set up for it. Did you used to have a bakery in here?"

"Not us, but maybe the former owners did. We only purchased this place about five years ago."

"Are there any ovens in here?"

"*Nee*, just the stove in the house."

"We could start out small. Just sell things like cookies, fry pies, things like that. Although I can make cakes and pies too."

"That's a good idea. Only, I'm not sure how they would sell, since we're kind of off the beaten path."

"Well, what if you offered fresh baked goods once or twice a week? You could put a sign out by the main road and that might drive traffic in."

"*Jah*, that sounds good."

"We can keep a little tray out and offer samples."

"I like your ideas."

"That's what I did back home. My *mamm* and sisters and I ran a bakery."

"I would need to talk to Silas about it, of course. We only have the one oven, so I'm afraid our offering will be limited."

"The best thing would be to have an oven inside the store, so customers breathe in the aromas of the cakes and breads and cookies the moment they step into the store."

"It sounds wonderful, but I'm afraid we'd have to do quite a bit of expanding to accommodate all that."

"Well, like I said, we could just start small. If it takes off, you'd have the extra income you need to expand."

Kayla shrugged. "I don't know. It would be one thing if you decided to move here permanently, but as it is, it's probably better if we just use what we have."

"I'm sorry if I'm overstepping my bounds. I just get excited when I see all this potential."

"Oh, no. I think it's a wonderful idea. I just hate to promise customers something and not be able to make good on it. Because, if you were to start it and then leave, there's no way I'd be able to keep up with it."

"I totally understand."

"We can still talk to Silas about it."

Jenny nodded, but her excitement deflated a little. Kayla was right, of course. If she didn't intend on staying, there would be no point in opening up a bakery. If she did, well, she'd need to find a place of her own. Because she was certain Silas and Kayla wouldn't want her hanging around indefinitely.

She sighed. It would be a long time before she could save up enough money to afford a place of her own.

"Would you mind arranging these outside too?" Kayla held up a couple of hanging flower pots and gestured to several more.

"Sure." Jenny smiled.

As she stepped outside, plants in hand, an Amish carriage pulled up. Two young women, near her own age, hopped down. The driver fastened the reins to the hitching post.

One of the young women smiled. "Hello, *ach*, you must be Kayla's friend from California. Sierra, right?"

Who was this woman and how did she know her?

"Paul told us all about you. I'm Silas and Paul's sister, Martha." She pulled the other woman close. "And this is my friend, Amy."

"Nice to meet you." Jenny smiled at the friendly young woman.

"She and Paul have been courting the past few months." Martha's smile widened. "Is he around?"

The smile disappeared from Jenny's face. Paul was already courting someone? Why then had he asked her to go on a buggy ride? Why did they go on a walk? Why had she dreamt about kissing him? "Uh, yes. He and Silas are in the metal shop out back," she managed.

How foolish she'd been to let herself fall for someone who was already taken. Paul shouldn't have asked, shouldn't even have suggested a ride, if he was in a relationship. It was wrong. Did he think his *aldi* wouldn't find out?

And here she thought that Paul was...

She would not cry. She would not.

She blinked away the threat of tears and returned to the task at hand. She probably shouldn't stay here. Not if she was a temptation for Paul. What if they had kissed in the barn last night? She would not be the one to wreck another woman's relationship. Especially not with a man like Paul, who'd been kind and seemed caring. Had she been wrong about him?

About ten minutes later, the buggy and its occupants took off down the road. Not long after that, Silas and Paul entered the shop.

Silas moved to Kayla and the *kinner*, sweeping up little Judah into his arms. "We ready to eat lunch?"

Jenny continued stocking shelves, but she could feel Paul's eyes on her.

"I can bring out the sandwiches we made this

morning," Kayla said. "Jenny, we can close up for a few minutes and take a break."

She turned toward Kayla, purposely avoiding Paul's gaze. "Oh, no. That's fine. I can stay out here." She turned back to the shelf.

"You're sure?"

She glanced her way again. "Yes, absolutely. Everything is priced, so I don't think I'll have a problem figuring things out if we have any customers."

"Okay, then. I'll bring you out a sandwich." Kayla smiled.

"Bring me one too, please." Paul's voice echoed.

Jenny turned around. "No, you don't have to stay out here. Go enjoy your lunch."

"*Nee*. I want to stay." He cocked a brow.

"Okay," Silas said. "We'll see you guys in a bit then. Paul, help her if she needs anything."

Silas, Kayla, and the children exited the store and began walking up the driveway to the house.

"You could have gone." Jenny's lips pressed together.

"I'd rather stay here with you." Why did his voice have to sound so smooth and husky when she was attempting to be upset with him?

She shook her head. "Please don't."

Paul's voice wavered, sounding unsure now. "Jenny,

what's wrong? I thought we were going to be friends."

"That's probably not a good idea."

"Why? Martha didn't—"

She spun around, challenging him. "Oh, I don't know. Maybe the fact that you already have a girlfriend."

"What?" He frowned. "I don't have a girlfriend."

"Amy? The girl that was just here? Your sister said you were courting."

"She's correct. We *were* courting. We aren't anymore."

"Why would she tell me that, then?"

"She's upset that I broke things off with Amy. And she believes you are *Englisch* and will lead me into the world." Paul sighed, then stepped close and lifted her chin with his finger. He stared into her eyes. "I am not interested in *her*."

She felt herself tremble at his nearness. She swallowed as her gaze searched his. "You're not?"

His eyes begged permission and she couldn't stop herself from nodding slightly. His hand moved behind her neck and he dropped his lips to hers as her eyelids draped closed. The kiss was slow and sweet, and his warm hand on her neck felt heavenly, but it ended way too soon.

"You need never doubt me." He caressed her cheek with his thumb, then stepped away.

"Paul, I..." She shook her head.

"What is it?" His brow lowered.

"I don't know how this is all going to turn out. With Atlee, me being *Englisch*." She shrugged. "Is this..." she gestured between the two of them, "Are *we* a good idea?"

"I'm not exactly sure what is happening between us. And I honestly do not understand it myself." He shook his head. "I wasn't looking for a *fraa*, for someone to spend the rest of my life with. But you...I've courted many *maed*, but I've never felt this way about anybody. Is that crazy or what?"

She blinked. "A...a *fraa*?"

"I know. I shouldn't have said anything. I'm going to scare you away. But I just..." His voice trailed off and he stared at her.

"I...I honestly don't know what to say about that. We're practically strangers, Paul. Marriage is a huge commitment. I'm not ready for that. And I don't think you are either."

"I shouldn't have said anything."

"It's just that, with Atlee..." she frowned, unsure if she should reveal her past with Paul.

"I'm not Atlee, and I never will be. I couldn't imagine ever bringing you harm." He reached up, caressing her earlobe.

"I know. It's just hard for me to trust, you know?"

"I do. And I'm not saying that we need to get hitched today or this week or this year even. I know you need time, and I'm perfectly content to give that to you." He searched her eyes. "But will you pray about it?"

"I will."

"*Gut.*" He bent down and placed a slow tantalizing kiss on her cheek.

"Uh...hum!" Their heads sprung upward at Silas's throat clearing.

Paul groaned. "Why are you back already?" He frowned at his brother.

"We decided to join you two. I can see now that it was a wise move. Kissing *Englisch maed* in the store is not *gut* for business, *bruder*."

Paul chuckled. "Oh, I beg to differ." He winked at Jenny.

"*Jah*, how's that, *bruder*?" He handed each of them a sandwich wrapped in a paper towel.

"It creates an air of romance." He twisted his hand up in the air.

Silas snorted.

Jenny couldn't help but laugh.

"What's this all about?" Kayla walked in, holding the hand of a child in each of her own.

"I come into the store and find these two kissing," Silas raised a brow toward his *fraa*.

Kayla's smile grew even wider and she eyed Jenny. "Oh, really? And this kiss you speak of, it was consensual?"

Jenny dipped her head after a slight nod, her cheeks warming.

"I don't know about all these Amish boys choosing *Englisch* girls. We're going to create quite a stir, Sierra." Kayla winked at her.

"Oh, you've already created plenty of stir, *lieb*." Silas grinned.

She grasped his suspender. "Oh, so it's all my fault?"

"Absolutely." Silas leaned down and kissed Kayla's lips right in front of Jenny, Paul, and the children.

"It's always the women," Paul agreed with a chuckle.

THIRTEEN

Atlee's mood improved as soon as he spotted the buggy in the driveway. He knew that carriage well, it belonged to the Christner family. Had Jenny returned home? She would, if she knew what was best for her. He wasn't going to tolerate a woman who had no respect for him.

He picked up his pace and began jogging toward the house. He'd cut his run short today because he just wasn't feeling it. Everything had seemed to turn upside down since Jenny left.

He huffed up the back steps and burst into the mudroom, overdue for a glass of water.

"Atlee? Is that you?" His father's voice called from the living room.

"*Jah*. Just came back from a jog." He filled his glass at the sink.

"Come in here, please."

He stepped into the room, where both of his folks sat. Jenny's parents were present too. *What is this?* He frowned.

"Hello." He nodded cordially to Jenny's folks.

"Atlee, we'd like you to join us." His father gestured toward one of their hickory rockers.

"What's going on? Have you heard from Jenny? Is she back? Where is she?" He frantically looked around the room. "Is she...she's okay, isn't she?"

"We believe she is fine," Jenny's father said.

He blew out a breath and sat down.

"We're concerned." His father eyed him carefully. "About you."

"Me? What do you mean?" His brow lowered.

"We have reason to believe your and Jenny's relationship was not all that it should be. That it should have been."

"What are you talking about? Jenny and I haven't shared the marriag—"

His father's hand went up to stop him. "That's not what I'm referring to *sohn*, but I am glad to hear that is not the case."

He wasn't sure what this was about, but whatever it was—

"We have reason to believe there might have been physical abuse going on. And *that* is why she left the community."

His blood ran hot. *If Jenny did ever come back...*

"What are you talking about? Who is saying this?" He ground out the words through clenched teeth.

"It was an anonymous source."

He shot up from the rocking chair, clenching his hands at his side. "It's a lie. I love Jenny."

"*Sohn*," his father's voice softened, "we want to get you help."

"Last time I heard, love was not a disease. I don't need help. I need to find my girl."

His mother handed his father two prescription bottles. She looked him in the eye. "We found these in your room."

He shrugged. "So?"

His father's eyes squeezed shut. He couldn't tell whether he was just frustrated or praying. Knowing his father, it was probably both.

"Those. Aren't. Mine." His fingernails dug into his palms. He could smash somebody's face in right now. If he only knew who this *anonymous source* was.

"What were they doing in your room then?"

"They're my *Englisch* friend, Doug's. I'm just holding them for him." He hoped his father believed him.

"Why are you holding them?"

"He asked me to."

"So you won't mind taking a drug test then?" Jenny's father spoke up now.

"What? Don't you believe me? Dad? Mom? Are you *serious*? You're going to take the word of an *anonymous source* over your own son's?"

"Prove us wrong." His father challenged.

"No." He shook his head. "I don't have to play your stupid games. If you don't believe me, that's your problem." He turned an evil eye on all of them.

He needed to get out of there. He didn't have to stay and listen to this interrogation.

"Atlee, sit down," his father requested.

"No." He shot out of the house before his father, or anyone else, could stop him.

It was time to figure out where Jenny went. He needed to find her. If she was here, she could vindicate him. She could tell them they were all wrong. And that was exactly what she *would* do. Just as soon as he found her and brought her back home.

FOURTEEN

Paul charged into the house in search of his sister, Martha. She was going to hear it from him this time, that was for sure. How could she go and tell Jenny that he was courting Amy, when he'd clearly put an end to that? And she knew it.

Ugh. Well, at least he'd gotten a kiss out of it. And maybe an understanding of sorts.

But still. It hadn't been Martha's place to say anything. It upset Jenny. And he hated seeing her distressed after all she'd already been through. She needed a safe haven, not more emotional drama.

When he didn't find her in the kitchen, he hollered up the stairs, "Martha!"

"She's out with the laundry, Paul," his younger sister Emily informed him.

"Oh, hey, Em." He tweaked her cheek. "Did you have a *gut* day at school?"

"Except for Timmy Stolzfoos teasing me and Bailey." She frowned.

"Sounds like he might like you girls."

"*Nee*, he hates us."

"Sometimes boys tease girls because they like them."

She thrust a hand on her small hip. "Why would they do that? It doesn't make any good sense. And it just makes the *maed* upset."

"Likely he's doing it for attention. Try talking to him at a normal time when he isn't teasing. You might just find that if he gets attention another way, he'll quit teasing."

"I guess I can try. But I don't think Timmy will ever quit teasing."

"He'll grow out of most of it eventually. But you're probably right." He winked at Emily, then continued outside in his pursuit of Martha.

He spotted her at the clothesline, removing laundry.

"What were you thinking today?" he blurted out.

"What do you mean, *bruder*?"

"You know. Telling Jenny I was courting Amy."

Her head shot up and she stared at him. "Jenny? Who's Jenny?"

"*Ach*." He shook his head. "Not Jenny, Sierra, I mean." He could kick himself for letting her real name slip out.

"Why?" Martha's lips curved into a smile. "Did Sierra get jealous?"

"No. I got mad." He firmed his arms across his chest.

"I didn't lie. I said you *were* courting her, which you *were*."

"What was your intention in telling her that? To ruin my chances with her?"

"Paul. Open your eyes, would you? She's *Englisch*. It's not like you actually have a chance with her."

He felt like hollering, *she's not Englisch!* But he couldn't. Jenny needed his protection right now. And if pretending she was *Englisch* would keep her safe, then that is what he would do.

"What do you know?" He shook his head. "Look at our older *bruder* and his *fraa*."

"It was different with them, and you know it. She needed him and he needed her. Totally different situation." She rolled her eyes. "And did you see what she was wearing today?"

"Maybe I need Sierra too. And maybe she needs me." He adjusted his stance. "And I thought she looked good. And don't gossip."

"You would." She sneered. "With a tight shirt like that..." Her brow lifted and she shot him a reproving look.

He did admit to himself that he found her *Englisch*

clothing attractive. And that he probably shouldn't. "Listen, just stop, okay? It's hard enough for her being here as it is. She doesn't need you sticking your finger into the pie."

"You really have it bad for her, don't you?"

"Thanks for stating the obvious."

"Well, good luck convincing *Mamm*."

"I don't have to convince anybody."

"Paul, why can't you just pick an Amish girl? Why do you have to bring the *Englisch* to our people? You know they will corrupt our ways." She unclipped the last towel and folded it, before dropping it into the basket. "What if I chose an *Englisch* man?"

He shrugged. "I guess if he's willing to become Amish, there isn't anything wrong with it."

"So you're saying Sierra is willing to become Amish? For you?"

"I don't know. Maybe, eventually." He hefted the laundry basket for her and they headed toward the house.

The moment they stepped into their home, *Mamm's* brows flew upward. "What has you two in a dither today?"

Just as Paul was about to utter *nothing*, Martha took the lead. "Oh, just Paul's *Englisch* girlfriend."

Oh no, here it goes.

"*Englisch* girlfriend?" *Mamm's* voice rose a pitch.

Martha smirked at Paul, whisked the laundry basket from his hands, and kissed his cheek. "You're welcome."

"For nothing." He growled.

"*Ach, nee.* Not again. Not you too," *Mamm* lamented.

"Yep. A friend of Kayla's from California," Martha volunteered, as she carried the laundry toward the stairs to be distributed in the *kinner's* bedrooms.

"Martha, *geh*!" Paul chased his sister to the stairs, and she screamed. She'd nearly dropped the basket as she skittered up the steps. Served her right. Although, if she'd actually spilled the contents, Paul was sure *Mamm* would demand *he* be the one to pick it up.

"Paul Miller! What is all this about?"

"I'll tell you what it's about. My *schweschder* won't mind her own beeswax," he made sure to holler the words up the stairs.

"Paul!" *Mamm* huffed.

"I'm tired of it, *Mamm*. Sheesh! Now I know how Silas felt and why he was willing to leave the Amish to marry Kayla."

"What? Now you're talking about leaving for this *Englisch* girl?"

Ach, he needed to diffuse this situation before he

gave his mother a heart attack. Because, technically, they were arguing over something that didn't even exist. Jenny wasn't *Englisch*. "No. I'm pretty sure she'll become Amish. I just wish everyone would let me make my own decisions, even if you think they are bad ones. I don't interfere with your choices, do I?"

"*Nee.* But I would hope that if you saw us going the wrong way, you would warn us of the dangers."

"Warn, *jah*, but not prod with a hot iron." His fists clenched. "Martha has already made her disagreement clear, which is why she needs to keep her trap closed now."

His mother frowned. "What happened to Amy? She was a nice *maedel*."

"Thank you," Martha's voice sang from upstairs.

Paul grunted. "Amy and I were just friends. I don't like her in a romantic way."

"Romance isn't everything, Paul. Perhaps you're infatuated with this new *Englisch maedel*, like a *bu* would be with a shiny new toy."

Paul rolled his eyes. *Seriously*? "*Mamm*, I'm twenty-two. Old enough to know the difference, don't you think?"

"The heart can be deceived at any age, *sohn*."

"You know what? I envy Silas. At least *he* had the *dawdi haus* he could escape to and didn't have to put up with all these women."

Mamm jammed a hand on her hip. "*All these women* are the ones who keep you fed and clothed. You'll do good to remember that. And you are bordering dangerously close to disrespect with your comment, young man. You'd be wise to watch your tongue."

Ach. "I don't mean any disrespect, *Mamm.* I just want to be my own man."

"You're of age. You are welcome to move out any time you wish." *Mamm* gestured toward the door.

"Into the *dawdi haus*?" Paul's brow quirked.

"We've already discussed that option."

His excitement deflated. "Well maybe I'll move in with Silas, then."

Martha charged down the stairs at that moment. No doubt she'd been eavesdropping on the entire conversation from upstairs. "You want to *move in* with your *Englisch* girlfriend, now?" Her voice practically screeched.

Paul sighed and plowed his fingers through his hair. *Ach*, they were driving him crazy! "Maybe I do," he retorted.

"Well, you can be sure the deacon will be on your doorstep in no time, if you choose that path, *sohn.*"

Of course, they'd snitch.

"You know that is not our way. I'm afraid this

Englischer is already having too much effect on you. And it's not *gut* that she's staying in that *haus* with a married couple. If she's already tempting you, who is to say she won't tempt your *bruder* as well?"

"Seriously, *Mamm*? How can you make these judgments about someone you've never even met? And there is no law saying a friend can't come to visit."

"Well, if she's just visiting, that means she should be gone soon, right?" Martha poked her nose in. Again.

"How long is she planning to stay?" *Mamm* frowned.

"I don't know." What was *wrong* with him? Why did he keep standing here arguing with unreasonable women? Jenny would have been way better off if he'd said nothing at all. Now, *Mamm* and Martha seemed bent on running Jenny off. Ugh. "I'm leaving now."

He had a plan. He didn't know if it was a good one or not, but it was worth a try. He stepped out into the fresh air, reveling in the calming effect it had on his nerves. He breathed in deeply, whispering a plea to *Der Herr*. Now, it was time to put his plan into motion.

FIFTEEN

"*D*at?" Paul walked into the barn.

"*Ach*, Paul. Just who I wanted to see. Will you check Ol' Charlie? I think he threw a shoe."

"Sure, *Dat*." He moved to check the horse's hooves, then fetched his farrier tools along with one of his pre-formed Ol' Charlie-sized horse shoes.

Dat's brow arched as he brushed down Ol' Charlie. "You wanted to ask me something?"

"*Jah*." He sighed. "Any chance you would allow me to rent the *dawdi haus*? I...need my own space."

"Does this have anything to do with that *Englisch* girl you're interested in?"

"You know about her?"

"Are you surprised? Between your *mamm* and your *schweschter*, I'd say half the *g'may* knows by now." He chuckled.

"*Jah.*" He shook his head. "I guess I shouldn't be surprised." And, of course, Amy knew too.

"You know they never could keep a *gut* story to themselves."

He sneered. "You're right about that."

"Did you ask your mother about staying in the *dawdi haus*?"

"Not exactly. But you know she doesn't approve." He grimaced.

"The only thing I worry about is it making more work for her."

"I would think she'd have less work if I'm the one keeping it clean. And I don't mind washing my own sheets and stuff."

His father eyed him curiously. "Have you ever used the wringer washer?"

"*Nee*, but I can learn. How hard can it be?"

His father chuckled, then shrugged. "Don't know. Never had to use one. Seems like we men get a mite spoiled sometimes."

"*Jah.*" Maybe he could talk Jenny into showing him how to use it. That might be fun, actually.

"It's fine by me, although I'll probably hear flak from your *mamm*."

"Really? You'll let me?"

"You're old enough to know your own mind on a

thing. So long as you abide in the Amish way."

"Thanks, *Dat*. As soon as I'm done with Ol' Charlie, I'm going to move my stuff over."

"Might be best to wait until your *mamm* goes out for a visit or shopping. That way, you can have it done by the time she gets home and you won't have to listen to any of her protests."

"*Ach*, you're right. Any idea of when she's going out next?"

"I believe she'll be doing some shopping tomorrow, in fact."

Tomorrow. He could wait another day. "I will wait then."

"And about the rent. How about we use a barter system? Maybe just exchange some shoes and one of your metal ornaments every now and then? I'm sure your *mamm* would appreciate one of those fancy windchimes you've fashioned." His eyes twinkled.

"I already shoe your horses for free. And you know I'd gladly give you a windchime."

"A workman is worthy of his hire, son. Besides, I think your money might be better spent saving up for a place of your own, ain't so?" *Dat* winked.

"*Ach, jah*. For sure." His grin widened. "*Denki, Dat*. Thanks a lot."

Jenny sighed in relief as she watched the *Englisch* driver of the truck drive away with Mr. Sanderson's vehicle on his trailer. That was one less thing to worry about.

She helped Kayla put the last of their simple lunch on the table, then sat down and waited for Silas to finish the silent prayer. It had been quiet without Paul around today and she missed his presence more than she would have imagined.

"Paul suggested something and I wanted to ask your opinion about it." Her gaze bounced from Kayla to Silas.

Silas nodded for her to continue.

"He suggested changing my name legally." She sighed. "He reasoned that if I did become *Englisch*, Atlee wouldn't be able to find me. Also, the leaders wouldn't need to contact my bishop to see if I'm in good standing."

Silas looked to Kayla, then at Jenny. "How do you feel about this?"

She shrugged. "I don't know. I mean, I think Paul is right about all that. It's just, I feel like it's all dishonest, and I don't really even want to be *Englisch*. And then to have to go through everything to become a member of the church again, when I am already a member of the church...I don't know. It just seems like a lot of trouble."

"Well, there's something else to consider too." Kayla took a sip of her tea. "They wouldn't let me join the church as an *Englischer* here."

"What do you mean?"

"I had to go to a more liberal *g'may* in Pennsylvania and join there under Bishop Judah Hostettler. After I became a member there, then Bishop Bontrager let me transfer here."

"Wait. Did you say *Bontrager*?" Her heartbeat sped up.

"*Jah*. Why?"

"*Ach, nee. Nee, nee, nee.* Atlee's last name is Bontrager. They are likely related. I can't join the *g'may* here."

Silas and Kayla stared at each other. "That could be a problem." Silas frowned.

"What am I going to do?" Her face sunk into her hands. "I need to leave."

"No, you don't," Kayla assured. "You can stay here. You don't have to attend church. At least, not until it is safe."

"And that's the thing. When will it be safe? If I know Atlee, he's out looking for me right now. He's not likely to stop until he finds me. When will I know it's safe?"

Kayla reached over and squeezed her hand. "I don't know the answer to that. But I do know that you have no car, no money, and nowhere else to go. You don't really have much of a choice."

Little Shiloh began to squirm, and Silas picked her up.

"Down," Judah begged as he saw Silas standing up.

"*Nee*, you must eat your food first. Sister needs a diaper change." Silas disappeared from the room with Shiloh in his arms.

Jenny smiled at Kayla. "He seems like a *gut dat*."

Kayla nodded. "The best. But he did need a little training at first."

"How so?"

"He did *not* want to change diapers. I insisted, because I might not always be around to do the job. Now, he doesn't seem to mind at all."

Jenny brought the conversation back to their original topic. "What would you do if you were in my shoes?"

"I think I would just keep on doing what we're doing. If something comes up that prevents us from continuing, we'll make adjustments. But until then, you're safe here. Nobody is insisting that you leave. You have a roof over your head, a place to stay, food to eat, and friends."

Jenny smiled. "What more do I need, right?"

"I think it is enough for now." Kayla patted Jenny's hand.

SIXTEEN

This had been one of the most bizarre days of Paul's life. Was it possible to be ecstatic and miserable all at the same time? Inside he'd been aching to see Jenny, in fact, he'd barely thought of much else since meeting her. But being able to move out of his folks' place was beyond fulfilling.

Ach, he could be his own man now, as opposed to being subject to his *mamm's* notions. He could come and go without being questioned. He could maybe even bring Jenny over without first getting his folks' approval.

He surveyed the *dawdi haus*—his very own dwelling. He felt like spinning a cartwheel, but he didn't think there was enough room in the small house. The house that now contained all his possessions. This was going to be *wunderbaar*.

His stomach growled and he suddenly realized he

hadn't eaten since breakfast. As soon as *Mamm* and his *schweschdern* had left for the store, he'd gotten busy and made quick work of moving his things out. He'd completely forgotten about food until now.

What time was it anyway? He glanced at the wall. *Ach*, there was no clock in the *dawdi haus* anymore. Silas must've taken it with him when he'd moved into the Yoders' old homestead with Kayla. The clock had been an engagement gift from Silas to his first wife Sadie Ann, who'd passed away a couple of years before he and Kayla met. Paul couldn't imagine being married to the love of his life then losing her so soon after marriage. His brother had grieved deeply for the *fraa* and *boppli* he'd lost, but he was eventually able to open his heart again to love Kayla.

He stepped into the main house, surprised to see his family, already around the supper table, and eating.

"*Ach*, you should have called me." He glanced at his usual seat at the table, but his setting was missing. His younger brother now occupied the spot he'd sat in just this morning. He frowned. What was going on?

"You have your own place now. You are responsible for your own meals." Were those smirks on *Mamm* and Martha's faces?

"Fine." He moved to the refrigerator.

"You are your own man now. It looks like you will need to hire a driver to go get your own groceries."

Seriously? He slammed the fridge door closed, then stomped back into the *dawdi haus*. He could have sworn he heard snickering at the table.

Ach, he had no food here. It was a little late to call a driver for a ride to the grocery store. At least Silas and Kayla owned a small store that carried essential grocery items. It was closed now, but they'd open it up for him. He'd just hitch up the horse and buggy and make a trip down the road. He'd been aching to see Jenny anyway. This was the perfect excuse.

Jah, it was a great idea after all. *Thanks, Mamm.*

The unmistakable sound of a horse and buggy entering Silas and Kayla's driveway caused Jenny to move to her bedroom door to see if she could figure out who their guest was. She didn't think Silas and Kayla were expecting company this evening. If they were, they hadn't mentioned anything to her.

"*Onkel* Paul's here," Bailey's voice called, likely to the other *kinner*.

Jenny automatically glanced down at her clothes, then ran her hands over her hair. She didn't want to seem too anxious, yet she coveted Paul's winsome smile. Was it wrong to covet smiles?

"Sierra," Kayla called for her.

She opened her door and stepped out. "Yes?"

"Paul just showed up. There's a good chance he'll want to see you." Kayla winked.

"Okay." She tried to ignore the fluttering inside her chest.

As she and Kayla entered the living room, she spotted both Silas and Paul sitting down. Silas on the rocking chair and Paul on the couch. The moment Paul turned his head and met her eyes, his lips curled into a gorgeous smile. It was like they were the only two people in the room—like time had stood still a fraction of a second while they communicated with just a look. *Ach*, she practically melted into a puddle right there in the middle of the room.

Surely, this was who *Der Herr* had chosen for her. Never in her life could she have imagined the sheer aching in her soul at the sight of this man.

It was in that moment that she knew. She had to tell him about her past. He had to know. Everything.

"We have a customer, it seems." Silas eyed his *fraa*.

"Who? Paul?"

Paul gestured for Jenny to sit next to him on the couch. "*Jah*. I've got good news. I moved out today."

"Out? Where?"

"Into the *dawdi haus*." He grinned.

"You finally talked *Mamm* into it, eh?" Silas chuckled.

"No way. I went to *Dat*. He agreed that I was responsible enough to have my own place. So here I am, being responsible."

"I don't get it." Silas's lips twisted.

"*Mamm* said that if I was going to be my own man, then I could make my own food. Didn't even set a place for me at the table tonight."

Silas hooted. "Didn't see that coming, huh?"

Poor baby. "I could fix you something up," Jenny offered.

Paul looked at her like she was the most wonderful person that ever lived. "That would be amazing. But that's not why I'm here. I came to get groceries to *keep* myself fed."

"Groceries? You're going to need more than that, baby *bruder*."

"Like what?"

"How many pots and pans do you have in there?"

"*Ach*, I didn't check."

"Well, I took all my stuff out, so unless *Mamm* restocked it..."

"*Ach*, I guess I'll need those too."

Silas rattled off a list. "And a spatula and a stirring spoon. Plates, cups, silverware, coffee pot."

"*Ach*, I didn't realize I'd need all that."

Silas nodded. "That and more. Is there any furniture in the house?"

"*Nee*, just my bed. And my desk and chair."

"You're going to go broke, *bruder*."

"I'll call it an investment for the future. Because I will need it when I take a *fraa* anyhow." He glanced at Jenny and warmth moved through her entire being.

"In that case, you should take a woman shopping with you. They have different tastes than we do. And they'll have a better idea what you'll need in a house."

He tossed Jenny a look and raised a single brow. "You game?"

"Sure. But I don't think Silas and Kayla have all of that in the store."

"No, we don't. But you can buy what you need to get you by," Kayla said.

Paul's head lifted. "Do you have any hickory rockers left? That's something I can't get at the other stores."

"One or two, I think." Kayla looked to Silas for confirmation.

"Do I get the favorite brother discount if I buy two?"

Silas chuckled. "Something like that. But I'll have you know that I don't have a favorite *bruder*." Silas pointed at Paul.

"I'll get what I can tonight, then maybe hire a driver tomorrow, if that works for you." His eyes meandered to Jenny once again.

"Can we go after the store closes? I'm a working girl now, you know." Jenny smiled.

"Sure. There should be plenty of daylight left." Paul reached over and lightly massaged her hand. "And maybe we could find a place to eat supper."

"Paul Miller, you know you're going to make people talk," Silas warned. "Running around with an *Englisch* girl."

Paul chuckled. "They're already talking. We're just going to give them something a little more exciting to talk about." He winked at Jenny, then squeezed her hand.

"You're not going to kiss her in public, are you?" Silas's eyes widened.

"Oooh, I hadn't planned on it, but that's not a bad idea." The look he gave Jenny reassured her he was only teasing. He leaned over and whispered in her ear, "I'd never embarrass you in public."

"Shall we check out the store, then?" Silas eyed his brother.

"Lead the way, *bruder*."

SEVENTEEN

Paul slid into the truck cab next to Jenny, then closed the door. "Thanks for giving us a ride, Joe."

"Sure, no problem. You said you wanted to go to Madison, right?" He slapped his blinker upward to turn left onto the main road.

"*Jah*. We need to do some shopping and I'd like to take Sierra out to eat."

"Okay, sounds good. What do you want to do first?" Joe glanced his way.

Paul turned to Jenny. "Are you hungry yet?"

"I could eat." She appeared as enthusiastic about this trip as he was.

"Let's go eat first, then. What do you recommend, Joe?"

"Are you looking for a sit-down restaurant or a fast-food joint?"

"Sit-down."

"Okay, well, let's see. Upper Madison or lower?"

"Probably something along Clifty Drive, since we'll be shopping up here."

"There's Ponderosa, Frisch's, Bob Evans, a couple of Mexican restaurants, Chinese food, a Japanese place, Pizza, and, uh, oh yeah, Harry's Stone Grill. My favorite."

"Never been there. They have good food?"

"Delicious."

"Okay, let's go there then." He turned to Jenny. "Does that sound good?"

She nodded.

"They're a little pricey," Joe warned.

"That's fine." Paul grimaced inwardly, but he was happy to spend money on Jenny. In fact, he felt like giving her the world. If only his pocketbook could afford to. This would be an expensive excursion.

"Okay, then. Harry's it is." Joe turned to look at him. "You know, I don't think I've ever seen any Amish at Harry's, now that I think about it."

"Yeah, we tend to prefer buffets. Like 88 King Buffet or Ponderosa."

"The thing about buffets is you get to try a little of everything."

Paul glanced out the window as they passed by the proving grounds. He always wondered what type of activities went on inside the fenced wooded area.

"What do you recommend at Harry's?"

"Not their coffee. Nah, go to Hos if you want that." Joe chuckled. "But with food, you can't go wrong. The mahi mahi is great, if you like fish."

Jenny grinned. "I love fish."

"Tender, flakey, flavorful, mmm...it's really good." Joe shook his head. "I can practically taste it."

Paul chuckled. "Maybe we'll both get it, then."

"My wife and I usually order two different things, eat half, and then switch plates. That way we both get to taste what the other is having."

Paul eyed Jenny. "Not a bad idea."

Joe turned onto Clifty Drive.

"Okay, I'll drop you two off then and pick you up in about forty-five minutes. Will that work?"

"Sure. That sounds *gut*."

"Then after that, where?"

"I need a couch, and some house stuff."

"Either a furniture shop, or they have a nice selection of furniture at Big Lots. There's also Walmart, of course."

"Maybe Big Lots, then Walmart, if that's okay?"

"Works for me." He pulled into the parking lot and stopped in front of the restaurant. "Have fun, you two."

Paul grinned and slid out. "We will."

Jenny followed, then shut the door and they waved him off. "Mm...it smells good, doesn't it?"

"My stomach is already doing flips." He reached for her hand, then thought better of it. He'd promised not to embarrass her in public. Instead, his hand dropped to the small of her back as he guided her inside.

Several moments later, they were seated at a table.

Paul perused his menu, then closed it, eyeing all of the taxidermical art on the wall. "It looks like somebody enjoys hunting."

The waitress appeared at the table and jotted down their order, took their menus, then disappeared again.

Jenny glanced up at the bear Paul had been looking at, then her gaze moved around the room. "I'd say so. Do you?"

"I don't mind it. One nice-size deer provides quite a bit of venison for a family."

Jenny grimaced.

"Don't like venison?"

"Eating it is fine, but cooking it makes my stomach feel queasy."

The waitress placed their drinks, bread, and salads on the table.

"That's no fun." Paul cut a slice of bread and

offered it to Jenny. He watched with a smile as she slathered butter on it. "It can always be cooked out on the grill too, I guess."

"Paul Miller."

He set his slice of bread down and looked upward to see Bishop Bontrager standing near the table.

"Hello, Jerry."

"I see the rumors are true. This is the *Englisch* friend staying in Silas's home?"

Jenny looked to Paul, worry clearly creasing her brow.

"*Jah.* Sierra, this is Jerry Bontrager, our bishop."

Jenny attempted a wobbly smile. "Nice to meet you."

She quickly sipped a drink of her water, likely to provide a distraction.

Jerry nodded, then turned his attention back to Paul. "I plan to stop by tomorrow. What time would be good?"

Paul swallowed. "Uh, seven in the evening?"

"I prefer mornings."

"We can do seven in the morning, then. Silas and I don't usually start in the shop until eight."

"Very well. I will see you then." The bishop nodded, then walked toward the restaurant's exit.

"They're coming to see you about me." Jenny frowned.

"Most likely. Don't worry, I'll handle it." He hoped he sounded more reassuring than what he felt. The last thing he wanted was to give Jenny one more thing to be anxious about.

"You are already a member of the church, right?"

"Yep." He popped a bite of bread into his mouth. *Ach*, it was delicious.

"It's not going to go well."

He reached across the table and placed his hand over hers, gently rubbing, then let go to indulge in more of the *wunderbaar* bread. "Don't worry. It'll work out. You'll see."

He cut another slice and handed it to Jenny. "It's *gut, jah*? We should probably eat our salads too."

She nodded, then picked up her fork and took a couple of bites. She seemed to be deep in thought.

"It would be so much easier if..." her voice trailed off and she glanced around.

"If you were Amish?" He whispered.

She dipped her head. "What are you going to say to him?"

"I plan to pray about it and follow God's leading. I figure I can't go wrong that way." He covered her hand again. "It'll be okay. I'm willing to be put in the *Bann* for you, if need be."

"I don't want that for you, Paul."

The waitress brought their entrees and asked if they needed anything else, then moved to another table.

"I know you don't, and I appreciate it. But whatever is going to happen is going to happen. We only have so much control over things. It's best not to fret, okay?"

"I'll try."

"That's all I ask." His mouth salivated as the aromas from their food hit his nostrils. "Now, shall we enjoy our supper?"

EIGHTEEN

Jenny and Paul took the final shopping bags from Joe's truck and hauled them to the *dawdi haus*. They would organize everything and put all the purchases away after they saw Joe off.

Paul now lifted one end of the couch. "You sure you're up to this?" he asked Jenny.

"Yes, I've got it." She moved to the opposite end.

"Make sure to lift with your knees, not your back," he advised.

"My knees, right." She lifted the couch.

Their driver chimed in. "Sorry I'm useless. If I hadn't thrown out my back a couple of weeks ago—"

"No worries, Joe. Sierra and I've got this. Right, Sierra?" He winked.

"You lead, I'll follow." She smiled.

He walked backwards through the door of the *dawdi haus*. "We'll just set it down here in the living room."

"Okay." Jenny set down her end, then surveyed Paul's living space. "Your place is cute."

"You're cute." His eyebrows raised twice. "I'll be right back. I need to pay Joe. Make yourself comfortable."

"Nope. Can't do that yet. We need to put all that stuff away first," she reminded.

"Right." He said, just as he stepped out the door.

Jenny began removing the items they'd purchased. She couldn't ever remember spending so much in one shopping trip. The couch alone was over three hundred dollars. And then with all the pots and pans and utensils and tableware, some of which he'd purchased the night before at Silas and Kayla's store, it was almost like they'd gone on a shopping spree. She hoped they'd thought of everything. It almost felt like they were a married couple choosing items for the new home they were setting up.

Except, they weren't married. And prior to meeting Paul Miller, just the prospect of marriage had been frightening. But now? With Paul? No, she shouldn't be thinking along those lines. Truthfully, she had no idea how long she'd even be able to stay here. If Atlee had any idea where about she was, he'd be knocking on every door in the vicinity and asking if they'd seen her.

She pushed away her worrisome thoughts and filled the sink with hot water and dish soap.

She heard Paul step back into the house at the same time she'd heard Joe's truck exiting the driveway. Her stomach did another flip-flop when he stepped behind her and clasped his hands around her waist. The warmth of his solid chest pressed against her back. *Ach*.

"What are you doing?" His voice was almost like a murmur in her ear and she could barely concentrate on the dishes she'd begun washing.

"Getting these ready so you can use them when you need to."

"You're washing everything?" He stepped back now, then stood beside her.

She longed for his closeness. "Yes."

"Why? I mean, I can see washing the stuff that's been out on the store shelves. But the stuff in the boxes? Nobody's touched them." *Ach*, just like a man.

"Maybe not, but they could have chemicals on them or cardboard dust or any number of things."

"Ah, I see. I guess I never thought about all that." He plunged his hands into the rinse water, removed a few utensils, and placed them in the drying rack she had insisted on purchasing.

"I don't know about you living here all alone, Paul

Miller. It might be dangerous."

He bumped her shoulder. "You think so, huh? You wouldn't happen to know of anyone looking for a place to stay, would you? Because I think I might have room for one more." His low husky voice sent chills racing up her spine.

"Just what are you asking, Paul Miller?"

"You just let your mind wander, *schatzi.*"

Her body tensed and she frowned. "Please don't call me that."

He leaned back and studied her, his brow furrowed. "Is that because—"

"It just, that name reminds me of Atlee."

"I see. Then I will try to remember to not ever call you that. I don't want to make you think of him." He lifted her chin and she met his gaze. "I'm sorry."

She swallowed. Paul was so *not* like Atlee. "No, it's...*you're* fine."

"You're sure?"

She nodded.

"I think maybe I'll call you *liebling.* Or, oooh, *schnickelfritz?*" he teased.

She gasped. "*Schnickelfritz?*"

"*Jah*, you look about like a *schnickelfritz.*"

"I do not!" she protested, then flicked water his way.

"You are proving my point." He tsked. "Now I'm going to have to get you back."

"You wouldn't." She giggled.

"I love that sound."

"What sound?"

"This one." He moved his hands to her waist and began tickling.

"*Ach*!" She gasped. Her wet hands automatically went to his shirt and she dried them on him, all the while giggling. She wriggled from his grasp and ran out of the kitchen.

"Oh, no you don't!"

She shrieked as he charged toward her, circling the couch. She ran around to the other side, while he gave chase. Just as she was making another round, he hopped over the back and caught her. He grabbed her by the waist and brought her down with him on the couch.

She couldn't wipe the smile off her face. Fun was something she'd never really experienced with Atlee. *This* was how she'd dreamed a romantic relationship should be. Paul had her in his clutches, but she felt none of the fear she'd experienced whenever Atlee's hands grasped her. There was a gentleness about Paul. She knew he could be trusted.

"Now I've gotcha where I want you." He chuckled.

An impish grin brightened his face. He raised his fingers as though to instigate another round of tickle torture.

She squealed. "No, don't you dare!" Her chest rose and fell with each breath.

"No? Okay, then." He pulled her onto his lap, lowered her to the side, then brought his lips down on top of hers. He hadn't begun slowly this time. Instead, it seemed like she was water and he, a man dying of thirst. His lips briefly left hers to taste of her jawline and neck. His hands entangled in her hair, then moved to caress her neck and shoulders.

Why did kissing Paul Miller feel like the most wonderful thing in the world? Why did she feel like staying with him, not only tonight, but every night for the rest of their lives?

"Jenny?" He left her lips to catch his breath. His eyes flamed with desire, and she knew what he would ask next. "Do you want to—"

"Yes." Her heart beat so rapidly as he lifted her into his arms, she thought she might have a heart attack then and there. But, *ach*, Paul was so worth it.

A pounding on the door killed the moment.

"*Ach. Nee.*" He groaned. Had Paul cursed under his breath? "I don't want to answer that."

"You have to."

He let her down.

She kissed him passionately on the mouth one more time, then stepped back feeling a little dizzy. She helped refasten two buttons on his shirt and slid his one suspender back over his shoulder.

She cleared her throat and checked her appearance, then quickly returned to the kitchen to resume the work that had been abandoned. Her pulse eventually slowed to almost normal. Normal, she found, didn't exist around Paul.

She listened carefully as Paul opened the door that led to the main house.

Frustrated, Paul practically yanked the door off the hinges. He was surprised to see his father standing on the other side. "*Dat*? Did you...need something?"

"We heard some racket going on in here. Your *mamm* thought I should check up on you."

Of course, she did. He felt like rolling his eyes.

"*Jah*, we were...well..." Paul shrugged. Surely his face was aflame.

"You have a *maedel* here?"

"*Jah*." He clenched then unclenched his hands, attempting to dispel some of the adrenaline he'd worked up.

"The *Englischer*?"

He nodded.

"You like this *maedel*, ain't so?"

"*Ach, jah.* More than just about anything." He squeezed his eyes shut. "*Dat*, I've never felt this way about anyone."

"Do you love her?"

"I believe I do."

"*Sohn*, a *fraa* and family is a big responsibility."

"I realize that."

His father examined his face carefully, as though he could see right through him. "You must go about things in the *right* way."

"I, uh, *jah*. I will." He swallowed and absentmindedly scratched the back of his neck.

"You will not only need to provide for the physical needs of a family, but their emotional and spiritual needs as well."

He nodded. "*Ach*, I guess I hadn't considered that part much."

"Have you been seeking wisdom from above? Have you been reading the words in God's book?"

Where *was* his Bible, anyway?

"Not...uh, no." Shame filled him.

"You need to. *Thy word have I hid in mine heart, that I might not sin against thee.* Can't very well hide it in your heart if you don't know what it says."

"I think I know what some of it says." The passages on the lust of the flesh and fleeing fornication just happened to come to mind at the moment.

"We must be ever learning of *Der Herr* and His ways."

"You're right."

"Remember this, *sohn*. Either the Good Book will keep you from sin, or sin will keep you from the Good Book."

Ach. Is that why he'd nearly given in to temptation? "*Denki, Dat*."

His father nodded, then stepped back into the main house and closed the door.

Paul blew out a long breath. *Forgive me, Lord.*

He rejoined Jenny in the kitchen and helped put away the items that were still out. They worked in silence, both dealing with their own thoughts and emotions.

He glanced over at her and shame filled him. "I'm sorry, Jenny. I shouldn't have—"

"It's okay."

"*Nee*, we almost..." he swallowed hard. "Sinned. I-I wasn't thinking."

"*Jah*. It would have been a mistake."

A half hour later, he sank into the couch next to

Jenny and stretched his arms wide. "Now, all we need is a TV or laptop, a movie, and some popcorn."

A smile spread across her lips. "A movie?"

"Something we used to enjoy with Kayla before she gave up all her worldly contraptions and became Amish." He glanced at her. "Hey, Sierra. Why don't *you* have any of those *Englisch* contraptions?"

"I'm a minimalist," she said matter-of-factly.

Paul chuckled. "A what?"

She laughed. "That's what Kayla said to say if people ask nosy questions like that."

"What does it mean?"

"It means I like to keep my possessions to a minimum, keep things simple."

"Wow. You *almost* sound Amish." He joked. "Are you sure you don't want to convert?"

"I suppose the right person might be able to persuade me." Her fingers traced his jaw line, prompting a heart-pounding kiss.

He forced himself to break contact before things spiraled out of control again. "I think, maybe...should I take you back now?"

She nodded. "Probably a good idea, but I wish..."

"I know. I do too." His hands caressed the softness of her hair, then he pressed his lips to the side of her head. *Ach*, he couldn't seem to get enough of her.

"Someday, *Gott* willing, I want to make you my *fraa*. But until then, I think we should try to be more careful."

NINETEEN

Paul was still ruminating on the evening before, when the knock came at the door. It had to be the leaders. Surely they would attempt to put his relationship with 'Sierra' to a stop. After all, he was already a baptized member of the Amish church and had no business dating an *Englisch* girl.

He pulled the door open. "Hello, Jerry," he greeted the bishop, then looked beyond him to greet the other leaders. Except, they weren't present.

"It's just me." He totally disarmed Paul with his wide grin.

A sense of ease fell over Paul. He really liked their bishop and felt fortunate to have one who was understanding and compassionate. "Please, come in."

"*Denki.*" He stepped inside.

"May I get you something to drink? Coffee? A snack?" Fortunately, he had food in the *dawdi haus* since he and Jenny had gone shopping.

"Just water will be fine. *Denki.*"

"Please, have a seat." Paul gestured to the couch and two hickory rockers, then made quick work of bringing out two glasses of water.

"I bet you're wondering why I'm here alone."

"I am."

"I wanted to get a handle on the situation before bringing it before the other leaders."

Paul swallowed and nodded.

"This *Englisch* girl, you are dating her?"

"Yes."

"Do you seek to leave our people?"

"No, not at all."

"Yet, you want to entertain the world?"

"She is willing to convert."

"I'm sorry, Paul. But I don't think the other leaders will go for this."

"Why not? Kayla—"

"Kayla was an entirely different situation. Her *boppli* had an Amish *vatter*. It was only proper that she be raised Plain."

This made no sense. "So, let me get this straight. If Sierra and I were to make a *boppli* together, the leaders would accept her into the *g'may*?"

"Paul, you know that is not our way." Jerry clasped

his hands together. "They are worried that our people are becoming too worldly. If we continue to accept *Englischers* into the *g'may*, we will progressively lean toward the world. The *Englisch* have their own ideas about things, and I'm afraid they don't always mesh with the old ways."

"Are you saying that I would never be able to marry Sierra?"

The bishop sighed. "Paul, I am not the one who makes all the decisions. If it were up to me, I might consider it." Compassion filled his eyes. "I'm sorry, Paul."

This was not good enough. He would not accept this.

What had he read just that morning? *The truth shall make you free. God, is that what You want?*

Paul stared at the bishop. "May I confide in you about something? I mean, it would have to stay between the two of us."

"If you've committed a grievous sin or a crime..."

"It's nothing like that. But I need absolute confidence that what I tell you will not get out."

"What you are asking is no small thing, Paul. As with every matter, I would pray and follow where the Lord leads."

Was that good enough? *Ach*, it would have to be. Surely, the bishop would not jeopardize Jenny's life.

He could trust him. He was sure of it.

God, please let this be the right thing to do.

He took a deep breath. "I really need this to be confidential. Sierra, the *Englischer*..."

Jerry nodded for him to continue.

Paul squeezed his eyes shut. "Her life is in danger. She is hiding out here."

Jerry frowned.

"She is really Amish. Her Amish boyfriend was abusive, and she fled for her life. We are calling her Kayla's *Englisch* friend to protect her. Because, if a scribe or another member of the *g'may* reports who she is and that she is here, the bad man will come and find her."

Jerry scratched his beard. "*Ach*, I see."

"We are protecting her, like Rahab hid the Israelite spies. We thought that would be acceptable."

"I will not mention this to the other leaders, but I may seek advice on the matter. Generally speaking, of course."

"No one can know. *Please*."

"I understand, Paul. I realize the gravity of the situation. Your secret is safe with me." He offered a reassuring smile. "And as for you and 'Sierra' dating, I'll try to hold the leaders at bay."

"*Denki*. You don't know how much I appreciate this. If you could take it to *Der Herr* in prayer and we can find a solution, that would be *wunderbaar*."

TWENTY

Paul grasped the piece of copper tubing he'd planned to use for the windchime he was crafting, then marked the places where he would drill the holes. He'd had difficulty concentrating today. Thoughts of his conversation with the bishop alternated with daydreaming about his moments with Jenny the previous evening.

"*Bruder*? Are you there?" Silas's hand moved in front of his face, bringing him back to the present.

"*Ach, jah.*" He frowned. "How would you feel about installing a security camera in the store out front?"

"A camera?"

"I'm worried about when Jenny is working at the store alone."

"Sierra," Silas corrected. "Kayla's worked alone many times and hasn't had any issues."

"Well, Kayla wasn't on the run either."

Silas nodded in understanding. "Ah, I see."

"I'd pay for it."

"You really like Sierra, don't you?"

"More than you know. Last night, we almost..." *Jah*, he shouldn't have brought that up. What was he thinking? *Ach*.

Silas's arms planted firmly over his chest. "You almost *what*?"

"*Ach*, I shouldn't have said anything."

"Well, you did, so spill it."

"I think you already know." He hung his head.

"Paul!"

"I know."

"This is bad."

"I know."

"Just think about it a minute, *bruder*. If you had, if you *do*, and for some reason this does not work out, you will both be devastated. There is a reason *Der Herr* said the marriage bed is to be undefiled. It is much more than just a physical thing. It is emotional and spiritual too."

"Spiritual? How so?"

"For one thing, it is ordained by God. We are three-part beings. Body, soul, and spirit. Everything we do has an effect on every part of us, but especially something as intimate as *that*. *Der Herr* has given us strict warnings against sins of the flesh. You create a soul tie when you become one flesh with another person. Within marriage, it is a beautiful thing. Without marriage, not so much."

A soul tie? He'd never considered it that way. "So if we had, then she left, it would be like her taking a part of my soul with her?"

"It goes both ways. She'd also be leaving a piece of her soul, a piece of her heart, with you. Neither of you would ever be the same again."

Paul swallowed. "I hadn't considered all that."

Silas chuckled. "You usually don't in the heat of the moment."

Heat of the moment was right. "I want to marry her. And not just because of that. She's the one for me. We click. It's like we were made for each other."

"You know, that's all great. I'm happy for you. But there's something to be said for patience."

"I'm afraid that's one thing I don't have an abundance of. Which is funny. Because last week at this time, marriage was the furthest thing from my mind. It's absolutely crazy."

"It's amazing what a day can bring forth, ain't so?"

"*Der Herr* sure is full of surprises sometimes."

"They are surprises to us, but perhaps well laid-out

plans to Him. After losing Sadie Ann, I never dreamed I'd be happily married to another woman—an *Englsich* woman, at that—and expecting our fourth *boppli*."

Paul chuckled. "You certainly didn't waste any time."

"Why would I?"

"I have no idea." Paul smiled.

Jenny pulled out a handful of socks from the shipment they'd just received, used the sticker gun to price each one, then placed them on the appropriate rack. She enjoyed working in this little country store, but so few customers stopped in, she wondered if it was even worth Silas and Kayla's while to keep it open. Of course, sometimes they did get customers who bought several items at once.

With everything Paul had purchased the other day, she wondered if he had been their most lucrative customer. But then again, he received a discount on most of it.

Kayla had informed her that they had usual customers who came in for specific items certain times of the week. Like Sammy Eicher, an upbeat older fellow who had a constant craving for Kayla's pot pies.

He'd stopped in yesterday and introduced himself, along with his grandson Michael, his grandson's wife Miriam, and their young son, Mikey. They were Amish as well, but attended church in a nearby district. Michael had commented that he'd known Silas since they were youths.

She'd offered the customers samples of the zucchini bread she'd baked, which resulted in Sammy purchasing a few loaves. He'd also purchased the chocolate peanut butter cookies she offered samples of.

"You keep baking these, and I'll keep buying them," Sammy exclaimed. Just his infectious smile would surely disarm a madman.

She'd risen early and began baking before the sun appeared over the horizon. Energized by the mere thought of Paul, she'd been eager to use the baking supplies they'd purchased the previous evening. She'd kept her hands busy all day.

She knew Silas and Kayla would appreciate the extra income her baking would eventually bring in. Because, once the word got out, customers would be flocking to their door. Well, at least, she *hoped* they would. That was how it had happened back home. If you had a great product that people enjoyed and would consume, you could have loyal customers for life. *Mamm* had stated that more than once, and from her experience, it seemed to be true. And if you regularly provided samples of new items, they might return out of sheer curiosity.

The bell on the door told her another customer had come, so she set the box aside and rose to greet them.

"It's only me." Just the sound of Paul's voice sent her heart racing.

"There's no such thing." She smiled as she took his hand, leading her around the sales counter.

He pulled her close and brought his lips down on hers. *Ach*, she'd never tire of his nearness.

He leaned back. "You know, I have all that new stuff at my house, but I haven't a clue what to do with it. You wouldn't happen to know of anyone I could hire to give me cooking lessons, would you?"

"Hire?"

"Well, I don't suspect anyone would offer to do it for free." His brow arched.

"Hmm...sounds like you need a *fraa*." She playfully tapped his chest. "And if you hire someone, then decide you want to marry her, she might not want to become your *fraa* because then she'll be doing the same job for free."

"I'm hoping the *other* benefits would outweigh the

wages she received." He murmured close to her ear.

"Well, in that case, I *might* know of someone." Had she seen a car's reflection out the front window?

"*Gut*. Because I'll likely starve to death if you—er, uh—*someone* doesn't come over to help."

"Well, I certainly wouldn't want that." She stuck out a pouty lip.

"Change of subject." He chuckled. "I finished installing the camera. Hopefully that will deter any bad guys."

She doubted it would. At least, she knew it wouldn't deter Atlee. But she wouldn't think of him right now. He didn't know where she was, and she felt safe here—especially when Paul held her in his arms. If only she'd met Paul first and never had to deal with Atlee.

At the sound of a customer entering the store, they jumped back, putting proper space between them.

Jenny looked up.

Straight into the enraged eyes of Atlee Bontrager. "Well, well, well. If it isn't my *fraa*, Jenny Bontrager. Caught in the arms of another man."

"Atlee?" Jenny swallowed, her pulse racing frantically.

TWENTY-ONE

"*Fraa*?" Paul's heartbeat raced faster than a Kentucky Derby horse, as he eyed the stocky man in front of him.

Wait. Jenny was *married* to this Atlee character? *Ach, nee!* This could not be.

Disillusionment filled his entire being. Here she...and they almost...then he would have...*ach*...

"Paul, it's not what you think." Jenny's voice wavered.

"Oh, no. It's *exactly* what he thinks." Atlee sneered, then pulled something from his pocket. "I even have the papers to prove it." He opened up the paper and shoved it in Paul's face.

Paul's gaze bounced from Atlee to Jenny as he read what was, indeed, a marriage license. "You signed this?" He stared at Jenny, dumbfounded, demanding answers.

She nodded once, and the world seem to crumble around him.

No, this was not happening. All his plans, all his dreams of sharing a life together with Jenny, raising their children...gone in an instant. Disappeared forever. This *couldn't* be happening!

"She sure did." Atlee hissed, then grasped Jenny's wrist and pulled her to his side. "Which means she's all mine. She belongs to me. And if you know what is best for you, you won't interfere. Or, we can solve this another way," he challenged, cracking his neck from side to side.

"Paul, I can explain." She reached a hand out to him, but he stepped away.

He shook his head, hating the tears that pricked his eyes. This woman, this *wunderbaar* woman whom he'd thought was to be his life mate, was already *married*? How could she lead him on like that? How could she let him believe she was available, and interested in him?

"There's no need." He stared her straight in the eye. "How could you lie to me like that? I'm...I'm done."

Then he turned, his footsteps slow and heavy, as he walked out of the store without a second glance.

"Paul, no!" Jenny screamed.

"Paul won't save you this time, Jenny. No one will." Atlee proceeded to twist her wrist and brought it behind her back, resulting in a searing pain.

Her breath stole away for a moment. "Atlee, please!" She cried. "Stop, you're hurting me!"

"You don't know what hurt is, *schatzi*." His hot breath pressed against her ear as he forced her back against him and pushed her toward the exit. "You are my *fraa,* and I intend to take full advantage of that. You might be a little broken right now, but it'll be okay. It'll all work out. You'll see."

God, help me!

"Let her go!" Someone called from the entrance.

Jenny's head jerked up at the voice. It was the man Paul had been talking to at the restaurant—the bishop of their district. Two other men, whom she didn't recognize, stood with him.

Atlee released his hold and the color drained from his face. "Uncle Jerry? What are you doing here?"

Uncle Jerry?

"I heard that you received a phone call, and had gone missing afterwards. Your *vatter* was worried about you," the bishop said.

Jenny rubbed her wrist, attempting to dispel the pain. She hoped it wasn't broken.

Atlee's eyes bulged. "But how did you find me?"

"Let's just say I have my sources." The bishop smiled. "Your *vatter* is on his way, *sohn*. He will get you help."

"Help? I don't need help." He pushed through the cluster of men and flew out the door.

Jenny watched through the glass door in amazement as Paul and Silas tackled Atlee to the asphalt.

All the tension she'd accumulated over the past several days seemed to reach its zenith and she crumbled to the floor in a heap. She began sobbing as her mind went back to the not so distant past...

The building Atlee had taken her to was unfamiliar to her. "Where are we?"

"Surprise!" A wicked grin slithered across Atlee's face.

Jenny's gaze bounced from Atlee to the young Englisch *man with him. Confusion creased her forehead. "I don't know what you mean."*

"This is my Englisch *friend, Art. Art meet Jenny, Jenny meet Art." He turned to her. "Art is licensed to perform ceremonies."*

Jenny frowned. "Ceremonies?"

"Weddings."

Jenny's brow furrowed. "I don't understand."

"We're getting married today, schatzi.*"*

She shook her head. "But I—"

Atlee turned around and spoke to Art. "Will you give us a moment, please?"

"Yeah, sure. I'll just step outside. Let me know when you're ready. Try not to take too long, though. I have a lot on my plate today." As soon as the man disappeared, Jenny's heart began to pound wildly.

Atlee pinned her with a reproving stare. "We're getting married today."

She knew she had to tread lightly here. She needed to try to find a way to reason with Atlee. To change his mind. "But, what about the g'may? My *mudder will be upset if she doesn't get to attend the wedding." Truthfully, she didn't ever plan on marrying Atlee. She'd been trying to break things off with him since the first signs she'd seen of abuse.*

He sneered. "I don't care about your mudder. I'm *not marrying her."*

"But this isn't the way things are done in our community, Atlee. You of all people should know that."

"Are you telling me what I should know?" Anger flared in his eyes.

"Nee, it's just that—"

"We're getting hitched today, and that's final."

Dare she defy him? "I-I don't want to."

That *had been the wrong thing to say.*

Atlee put his hand to her throat, squeezed, and thrust her back up against the nearest wall, knocking her head in the process. Fury raged in his steely gray eyes. "You will *marry me today, understand?"*

Tears pricked her eyes and she could barely breathe. She attempted to pry his hand off her throat. She shook her head in defiance.

He grasped her hand with his free one and twisted it. She winced in pain, but couldn't cry out.

"You will say 'I do' when that man asks you to, and you will sign the papers without a fuss." His hold tightened. "Or else, I will make sure you never marry anyone. Do you understand?"

She believed he meant every word he spoke. Atlee made good on his promises. Was being married to Atlee worse than death? Jah, *probably. Maybe. But she wasn't ready to die. She wasn't ready to stand before* Der Herr. *She wasn't sure if she'd been* gut *enough.*

If she could just get through this and get out of this place, she would find a way to escape Atlee. Because, if she didn't agree to his demands, she was certain she'd never make it home alive.

Jenny nodded and attempted to say okay.

That was when he finally released his grip on her. She nearly collapsed, but Atlee caught her. His demeanor changed in an instant and he smoothed a hand over her brow. Almost like he cared. His voice softened. "I'm sorry, schatzi. I'm sorry. Forgive me. I love you. You know that, don't you?" He bent his head and kissed her lips.

How she loathed the games Atlee played. She didn't know if he actually believed himself or if he expected her to, but she agreed anyhow. Anything to avoid his recurring wrath and the anguish it brought.

At first, Atlee had seemed sweet. She'd been attracted to his toned, solid physique. He wasn't too tall, just a few inches taller than her five foot five. She'd thought he was good-looking enough for her to agree to a ride home from a singing. Then one ride turned into another, and here they were ten months later.

She should have broken it off with him months ago, at the first sign of his aggressiveness. She should have run in the other direction. Why hadn't she? When she tried to mention some of his actions to one of her friends, her claims had been downplayed and she'd been brushed aside. It didn't help that Atlee was one of the minister's sons. People in the community respected their family. His minister father was a favorite among the g'may. So she learned just to keep it to herself.

But this couldn't continue. She didn't want to be

189

married to Atlee. She didn't want to be with Atlee. All she could see was more pain and misery up ahead and that was not what she had envisioned for her life.

Why couldn't she just find someone who was kind and caring? He didn't need to be overly romantic or dashingly handsome. She just wanted someone who would respect her, someone who would love and protect her. Not someone who would cause her harm.

Not Atlee.

TWENTY-TWO

"Jenny? Are you okay, baby?" She lifted her gaze to Paul's wonderful face, his mien now remorseful. "Forgive me. I'm sorry I left you." He extended a hand to help her to her feet.

She sobbed into her palms. "He forced me to marry him! I didn't want to. That's why I escaped."

"*Ach*, Jenny. I'm such a *dummkopp*. I didn't realize..." He shook his head, obviously frustrated with himself.

He brushed her tears away with the pads of his thumbs, but refrained from kissing her, even though the others had gone outside.

"I thought he was going to kill me, Paul. I wasn't ready to die. I wasn't ready to stand before *Der Herr*."

He held her back and stared into her troubled eyes. "What do you mean by you weren't ready?"

"Because I haven't done enough good things. I

know I haven't. And especially now, since I've been deceiving everybody."

Paul's frown set in. "Jenny, no. That's not how it works."

"What do you mean?"

"God does not weigh our good deeds and bad deeds on a scale to see which one weighs more. It is not by works of righteousness that we are saved. Doing good deeds cannot make us right before *Der Herr*."

"They can't? Why not? Then how…?"

"Because God uses a different scale. You are on one side and Christ is on the other. Do you think you have done enough good deeds to surpass Christ?"

She gasped. "No, of course, not. Nobody has."

"That's right. There is none righteous. No, not one. We are all sinners and come short."

"I don't understand, then. How do we become right before God?"

"Faith."

"That's it?"

"*For by grace are ye saved through faith; and that not of yourselves: it is the gift of God: Not of works, lest any man should boast.* You see, salvation is a free gift that God wants to give everyone. But they must choose to place their faith and trust in Jesus Christ. *That* is why He died."

"So He died to *buy* our salvation?"

"Yes. Exactly. It was the bride price. The price required to purchase His bride. His blood washes away all our sin and gives us a clean slate with God. When we accept the gift, we become members of the church, the bride of Christ."

"I guess I never understood that. Thank you for explaining it." She frowned. "So, how does it work then?"

"The Bible says *that if thou shalt confess with thy mouth the Lord Jesus, and shalt believe in thine heart that God raised him from the dead, thou shalt be saved.*"

"It sounds too easy."

"I guarantee you it was not easy for Jesus. He paid the price for the whole world. It was a heavy price tag. But it is free for us, thank God. I guess you can say it's the most expensive free gift ever given."

"How did you learn this? Do they teach it in church here?"

"Not exactly." He grimaced. "I've learned from Silas. He studies the Bible with an *Englisch* friend who is a pastor."

She nodded in understanding. "I see. So do you think...should I pray? Is that what it means by 'confess with thy mouth'?"

"If you want to, absolutely." His grin widened.

He bowed his head and reached for her hand. She winced when he took it in his.

He glanced down at her wrist and grimaced in horror. "Your hand! I'm sorry."

"We can pray without holding hands." She bowed her head and prayed silently, then looked up and smiled. "I did it."

"Wonderful." He gently brushed his fingers over the discoloration of her hand. "You need to see a doctor."

"It's okay."

"No, it's not."

"We can just put ice on it. I don't think it's broken. I can move it. It just hurts really bad."

"I will never understand people like that." He growled.

The bishop walked back inside the store. "Atlee is taking a ride to the police station."

"The police?" Jenny's eyes flew open.

"He needs to know this is serious, and his behavior won't be tolerated," the bishop said. "They won't keep him. The officer said they might detain him overnight, then release him to his *vatter*. He will get counseling for his substance abuse and be required to attend anger management classes. The officer recommended a restraining order that will prevent him coming near you, Jenny."

"Substance abuse? Paul was right about the drugs then?" Her gaze bounced from the bishop to Paul.

She noted sadness in the bishop's eyes. "Unfortunately."

"He forced Jenny to marry him." Paul stated, his lips turned down. "That's when she fled."

The bishop eyed her. "Is this true?"

She nodded.

"A marriage under duress is invalid and should be easy to annul, then. We will see to that right away, if that is what you want."

"Yes, it is." She sighed in relief, as tears surfaced in her eyes. "*Denki.*"

"In the meantime, we will have a special members meeting. It seems like the subject of gossip is in dire need of addressing in this community. There are too many busybodies within our *g'may*. While it may seem like idle chatter, this time it has put our sister's life in jeopardy. *Whoso keepeth his mouth and his tongue keepeth his soul from troubles.*"

Jenny hated that she'd brought so much drama to this community.

The bishop continued, "I'm guessing we will need to vote on receiving a new member also, am I correct?" He studied Jenny.

She looked to Paul, attempting to read his expression. Did he approve? Did he still want her?

"Is that what is necessary for a wedding in the fall?" Jenny didn't miss the look of love in Paul's eyes. "That is, if Jenny will have me."

"*Ach*, Paul." She stepped into his outstretched arm. Right there, in front of the bishop.

She nodded toward the bishop.

"Very well, then I will leave you two to..." His eyes sparkled and he shook his head, then walked out the door.

"I love you more than you'll ever know." Paul lifted her chin, then brought his lips to hers in a soft, slow, sweet kiss.

Jenny closed her eyes and gave thanks to *Der Herr* for His goodness to her. Just knowing that Atlee was out of the picture now, and hopefully getting help, removed a tremendous burden from her shoulders. She felt vindicated and sad and happy all at the same time.

Now she was free to be herself—Amish Jenny—and no longer had to deceive anyone. And now, she was free to love handsome Paul Miller, who never ceased to amaze her with his charming ways. *Jah*, he'd disappointed her when Atlee showed up. He *was* human, after all. But she tried to put herself in Paul's shoes. How would *she* have reacted if she'd learned *he* was married? She couldn't even imagine the pain and betrayal she'd feel.

Gott had given her grace to forgive, not only Paul, but his sister who had come and confessed that after hearing Jenny's name slip from Paul's lips, she'd mentioned it to Amy. That was when Amy had realized who Jenny was—her second cousin Atlee's girlfriend whom she'd seen him with at a wedding months prior. She'd called Atlee to ask after her and that was when Atlee had discovered her whereabouts.

Amy and Martha had both sought forgiveness, not realizing the kind of turmoil that their actions would bring to Jenny's life. Neither of them had known Atlee and Jenny's past, so she'd somewhat sympathized with their plight. Both of the young women swore off gossip, especially after the stern reprimand they received from the leaders.

But *Der Herr* had set everything to rights. Jenny now knew that *Gott* was indeed sovereign and He could be trusted with every detail of her life.

EPILOGUE

Five months later...

"Kayla and I have been talking." Silas looked across the table, first at Paul, then to Jenny. "We were thinking of possibly building a *dawdi haus* on our property. You wouldn't know of anyone who might want to rent it, would you?"

"Rent?" Paul pressed his lips together. "I don't know. I was thinking it's about time I started looking to buy a place of my own, since I'll be taking a *fraa* soon." He winked at Jenny.

"In that case, I have *gut* news for you." Silas brightened.

"What's that?"

"I was just talking to our next-door neighbor. He's putting his property up for sale next month. He and his *fraa* are moving out-of-state to be closer to their grandchildren."

Paul grinned like a fool. "For real? Next door?" His eyes shot to Jenny. "That would be perfect. Jenny could use our oven for her baked goods, and bring them to the store fresh every morning."

"Yes! We've had a ton of orders since the weather turned chilly. You'll likely be baking around the clock from now till Christmas." Kayla nodded, holding two-month-old Sierra in her arms.

Jenny's grin broadened as her eyes moved from the precious *boppli* back to Paul. "And you could walk to work."

Paul rubbed his chin. "Do you know what he wants for it?"

"I don't, but I'm guessing it'll be affordable. They're looking for a quick sale. Do you have money for a down payment, if you need to get a loan?"

"*Jah*. I've been saving up as much as I can."

"I have been too," Jenny added.

"You want to walk over there and talk to him after supper?" he asked Silas.

"*Jah*, that'd be great. I'm sure the *maed* can handle it for a few minutes without us." He winked at his *fraa*.

Kayla looked to Jenny. "We can work on your dress."

"Or I can hold this sweet *boppli* while you work on

my dress." Jenny kissed the baby's head. "*Ach*, I still can't believe it."

"Believe it, *liebschen*." Paul reached over and squeezed her hand, which had healed nicely without a visit to the doctor. "Less than a month and I make you my *fraa*."

"I have a surprise for you!" Paul pulled Jenny along, as they walked down the road from Silas and Kayla's house. Their wedding had been absolutely *wunderbaar*, but he couldn't wait to be alone with his new *fraa*.

"Where are we going? And is this a good idea in the middle of the night? You never know, a crazy driver could come barreling down this road and crash right into us." She teased.

"*Nee*, I think that driver is off the road for *gut* now." He leaned down and kissed her lips.

They moved to the side as several buggies of young folks passed by, hooting and hollering as they went. Paul loved the excitement, fun, and games that accompanied Amish wedding ceremonies.

Soon, though, he hoped to see excitement on his *fraa's* face as he carried her across the threshold of their new home that he'd secretly signed papers on yesterday. Friends and family had been working feverishly to clean and ready it for their wedding night.

When they turned down the driveway, Jenny gasped.

"Yep! It's all ours now."

He saw her white teeth sparkling in the moonlight. "For real?"

"For real."

Silas had said they'd leave it unlocked. He lifted Jenny into his arms and twisted the knob. Except, the door only opened a smidgen, then closed again. *Ach.*

He set his *fraa* down. "Sorry."

"Look. There's a note on the door." Jenny peeled off the paper.

Paul attempted to read it by the moonlight. "Have fun on your wedding night, and try to get some sleep *if* you can. Ha! Ha!" He laughed, not sure he fully understood the meaning of the note.

Paul pushed the door open again, but still felt resistance. "This doesn't want to open."

He pressed against it enough to carefully stick his fingers through to try and figure out what was preventing the door from opening. Something bouncy met his fingers. *What on earth?*

"A balloon?" He frowned.

Jenny moved to the window. "You're not going to believe this. It looks like the entire house is filled with balloons." She laughed. "I guess that's what the note meant by try to get some sleep *if* you can."

"Do you have anything to pop these with?" Paul's lips smashed together, but he kept his comments to himself.

She removed two straight pins from her apron. "One for me, one for you."

"It's nice to know those straight pins come in handy for something other than holding your apron in place." He popped a balloon and something fell out.

"It's a note!" Jenny exclaimed. She picked the note up off the ground and unfolded it. She squinted as she read, "Be ye angry and sin not."

She popped another balloon. "Do you think there's a message inside all of them?"

Paul sighed. "I don't know, *liebschen*."

She leaned over and kissed him with fervor, leaving him longing for more. "You're so cute, husband."

"I can't believe this." Paul shook his head in frustration, half chuckling. "I'm going to kill Silas."

THE END

Thanks for reading!
Word of mouth is one of the best forms of
advertisement and a HUGE blessing to the
author. If you enjoyed this book, **please** consider
leaving a review, sharing on social media, and
telling your reading friends.

THANK YOU!

DISCUSSION QUESTIONS

1. The book opens with a near collision. Have you ever been in a car accident? Has a car accident affected your life?

2. Jenny felt she had to keep her past a secret. Have you ever kept a secret?

3. In spite of being a stranger, Jenny felt an instant kinship with Kayla. Have you ever met someone and knew right away you be good friends?

4. Paul and his brother Silas are forever teasing each other. Do you and any of your siblings (if you have any) have a camaraderie?

5. For Jenny's safety, Paul suggests something that involves deception. Do you believe it's ever right to use deception?

6. Martha jumped to conclusions partly because she didn't have all facts. Have you ever done that?

7. Do you have someone who meddles in your affairs? How do you deal with them?

8. Kayla and Silas own a rural Amish store. Do you have a favorite Amish store to shop at?

9. Jenny was more afraid of dying than being abused, because she felt like she wasn't ready to meet God. Do you feel you are ready to meet God?

10. Jenny was confused about salvation and thought that if she only did enough good works, God might accept her. According to Jesus in John 6:28-29 KJV, what work is necessary for everlasting life?

11. Who was your favorite character in *The Charmer*? Why?

A SPECIAL THANK YOU

Thank you to Amy Fields and Debbie Renner, members of my Facebook readers group, who had a hand in naming Sierra and Amy!

I'd like to take this time to thank everyone that had any involvement in this book and its production, including my Mom and Dad, who have always been supportive of my writing, my longsuffering Family—especially my handsome, encouraging Hubby, my Amish and former-Amish friends who have helped immensely in my understanding of the Amish ways, my supportive Pastor and Church family, my Proofreaders, my Editor, my CIA Facebook author friends who have been a tremendous help, my wonderful Readers who buy, read, offer great input, and leave encouraging reviews and emails, my awesome Launch Team who, I'm confident, will 'Sprede the Word' about *The Charmer*! And last, but certainly not least, I'd like to thank my *Precious LORD and SAVIOUR JESUS CHRIST*, for without Him, none of this would have been possible!

If you haven't joined my Facebook reader group, you may do so here:
https://www.facebook.com/groups/379193966104149/

Available NOW for preorder:

The Unexpected Christmas Gift
Featured in
Amish Christmas Miracles Collection

Release Date: November 10, 2020